Sleeping Beauty

AND THE BEAST

A NOVEL

Melissa Lemon

ISBN: 1499788800
ISBN-13: 978-1499788808
Cover design by Cindy Canizales

To Mom & Dad

Thanks for loving me

MAGNOLIA

Time is running out. I peer out the back window taking notice of the fierce wind, the dark sky strewn with hesitant rain clouds that release only a drop here, a drop there. They will be here soon, and I fear what they will do. My own life means little to me now; I think only of Ovinia. Even though I've seen it in vision, and know the outcome of her future, that does not stop me from trying to spare her the pain of it all.

How weary these implacable visions have become. I see too much. Know too much. And now, it is my own life that has been so cruelly impacted by them. Or did the visions come as a warning? Is it possible to evade what I have seen?

No, experience tells me they will come to pass, but I cannot accept that. Not now.

I pull the cloth snuggly around her, wanting her to be warm enough, and protected from the lashing wind. If only this act could protect her from everything else. I sling a pack of supplies around my shoulder, enough to keep us fed for a few days at least. Then I cuddle her to my breast, wrapping my cloak around her. She smiles up at me, so pure and innocent, so foreign to pain and discomfort, so ignorant of what she will have to endure if I fail now. I try to ignore the nagging in my mind that I am being foolish, that if I have seen it in vision there is nothing I can do to prevent it. Absolute foresight was the gift bestowed upon me when I chose to become a witch. I was promised that any vision I had would surely come to pass, and so far, this has been true. Still, she is my only child, and the mother in me forbids acceptance without at least trying.

A loud, forceful knocking sounds at the door, jolting me and instantly increasing the already rapid pounding of my heart.

I unlatch the large window and fling it open, sticking one leg through and crouching my head. I try to pull myself up with one arm, but it is useless. Holding Ovinia out from me—knowing she is bundled enough to protect her from harm—I drop her into the long grass, hoping they do not hear out front. A startled look forms on her face, and a pout, but she does not cry. I smile at her to let her know it is all right, and it works. She believes me. In her infant trust, she believes that all will be well, even though I know it will not. I slide out of the window and onto the grass, and then swoop her into my arms again. I begin to step away from the house, lightly at first, and then in a run. Their voices grow distant behind me.

"There she is!"

I may not be as young or as strong as they are, but I am fast, even with the baby, and at first it seems I am too far ahead for them to catch me.

One of them grows closer now, enough that I can hear his boots in the grass and his heavy breathing. I panic, for either they will take the child and kill me, or they will kill us both. No, that is not what I have seen. They will take her and . . . My heart beats furiously, but I am full of energy. I feel like I could fly, and for a moment I think I will lift off the ground and into the air, but then someone grabs my hair and jerks me to a painful stop. I slip and fall to the earth, and as Ovinia slips into an awkward dangling position, she begins to cry. I don't think she is hurt, just aware now that something is wrong; she feels my fear.

The man still holds my hair tightly in his grasp, pulling and pinching my scalp as I try to cradle her once more. "I've got her!" Six or seven men catch up to him, all breathless. I am no match for them, even with my powers. No matter what curses I utter, it will not protect her, only punish them; and her safety is my only wish. But they will take her, and then want to take me back to Fallund Square where I would be tried and hanged. I am one of the last to survive the witch hunt. For a moment, the faces of my friends who have already been put to death flash in my mind. Did one of them rat me out before being murdered? Or was it a suspicious villager who reported me?

One of the men forces Ovinia from my hands as I cling and protest from my knees, screaming and grunting until he slams the back of his hand across my cheek. I land face down in the damp grass.

"Here's the baby. Do we need to head back now? What time is the auction?"

"Her name is Ovinia." I push my hands into the cold, stiff ground, lifting myself onto my knees again.

They do not listen to me as they are still more occupied with catching their breath and deciding what their next move is.

"What do we do with this one?"

"Bind her. Take her back to the square."

A loud crack of thunder fills the sky, rumbling loudly while it travels on and on. As the rain begins to fall harder, the drops penetrate my head, cheeks and shoulders, dampening my hair and old dress. I close my eyes, reviewing in my mind all that I saw in vision: Ovinia's tragic life, my escape. I see her bringing water from a well only to be punished for losing a few drops from the bucket; her tormented eyes haunt my consciousness as she trembles fearfully in the corner of a house where she does not belong; I witness the lashes across her pudgy toddler hands, her child-sized back, her growing, changing face; I watch as she covers her ears, protecting them from screams that I will never actually hear or be able to prevent; lastly, I see the crimes she commits, the horrible beast she becomes. And even though I've seen it and know it will come to pass, I hesitate to leave her. I am her mother. My instinct tells me to take her back and run again, but I know that will be pointless. Whether I live or die, her fate remains unchanged, and so I may as well live.

It is necessary to shove Ovinia from my mind, and so I do, for only a moment I think of my own life, my own chance to get away from the punishment awaiting myself and every witch in Fallund who is caught. A growing despair begins to gnaw at me as I accept that no matter what I wish for Ovinia, it is hopeless now. And the pain of it, seeping into my heart, is cankering and unbearable. There is only one thing left I am able to do.

Opening my eyes, and careful they do not see, I raise one knee in preparation. Waiting for my next chance to move without being noticed, I lean forward. The time is now. The men have been reviewing a map and deciding whether to take the baby and me straightaway or whether to make another capture first. Currently they are hunkered underneath their jackets and the branches of a tree. Falling incessantly now, the rain has given me my chance. My heart pounding, my mind swirling with agonizing thoughts and misgivings, I glance to my babe once more, whose tender infant cry is almost drowned out by an angry clap of thunder. Turning from her, I burst into a run.

Faster and faster I go, the wind and direction of the rain seemingly helping my speed, for which I'm grateful because my heart is like solid metal, heavy and preventing. Whether they begin to chase me or not, I do not know. I only feel the pain of losing my baby, the constant yanking at my heavy heart, pleading me to go back and save her. And because I cannot answer these demands, it threatens to rip open. I begin to cry, the tears cold and wet on my skin. And then I am sobbing and gasping, but I do not stop running. My grief is too great, and the wind too loud for me to hear whether I'm being pursued, but I have seen it. I know that I escape. And so I run.

Finally, when I am confident I am alone, I slow down gradually until I have stopped. Falling into the grass, I lie on my back and look up at the sky, drenched and completely breathless. The wind shakes the soggy grass all around me, but the rain has slowed once more. I am panting and wheezing when it hits me all at once, the pain again. It fills me like a poison—the excruciating agony—and I cannot help but cry out for how much it hurts. I close my eyes, the tears flowing freely, the sobs escaping my lips. Watching my friends being captured one by one, and now being driven from my own home, none of it compares to losing my sweet baby girl.

Even more tormenting are the images from the vision. They are fresh in my mind now. She will be sold in Fallund Square. I picture him in the crowd, the man that will buy her, along with his wife and another kinsman. I already despise them because of the visions I've seen. But a hatred so real and so thick swells up in my breast as I think of them now, these people I've never met. It has an intensity that I have never known before. I think of how unjust it is, that I should be wanted for dead, when they will all take part in abusing and degrading my daughter. I want to kill them, and for another moment I consider going back to do it.

Then I remember the visions. I know no matter what I try to do, they will come to pass. It is hard to restrain myself, to keep from going back and trying to save her, but somehow I stay there in the grass and attempt to push the images from my mind.

As the rain comes to a complete stop, I realize who it is I am most angry with, who is most to blame for the tragedy that will be my daughter's life, and the nothingness that will be my own: the king of Fallund. He is the one who ordered the witch hunts. He is the one whose paranoia caused contention where there was once a passive relationship.

Knowing I can never go back to my home, I rise once more, running and running until I reach the border of Fallund and Cray. It is difficult to cross the line into another country. It is saying the goodbye I could never be prepared to say. I hold one foot over the river that divides the land, still hesitant, a part of me still wanting to go back and get her. I consider this idea. If I take her at night perhaps I could get away without being caught.

I shake the thought from my mind. I have seen it. Nothing I do will change what I have seen in the vision. I wonder how often I will have to remind myself of this fact over the years, how many times I will have to convince myself that rescuing her is not possible. She will have to endure it all. I will have to move on without her.

I step into the icy water. It runs over my foot, cruel

and unfeeling, unsympathetic to my troubles. Instantly, a stiffening numbness consumes me, body and soul. Splashing across the river as I lift the hem of my dress, I begin to cry again. I hate them. I hate them all. As the freezing water penetrates my very bones, a fire ignites in my heart, a craving for justice, followed by an idea. I will punish the king of Fallund!

I run across the open grassy field and into the neighboring country. I know this is my home now, no matter how much it feels strange and unwanted.

Her smile comes to my mind, and those bright eyes that I know will grow so dim over time, so hateful. And yet another thought comes to mind, the source of which I cannot tell. Perhaps my heart is reaching down deep for a hope that my head cannot fathom. Even after all I've seen, I am suddenly optimistic that I will see her again. It is only an inkling, but a promising one, and heartening too. Then it flees away, and I am met again with the bitter sorrow of a mother who has lost her only daughter. That is soon replaced once more with a fiery anger and a pledge to avenge.

The clouds part in time for me to glimpse the setting sun, and with every step it grows darker, until I find myself in the darkest wood I have ever seen, a wood so dark

I know it will be the birth place of my nightmares.

1

Beauty

It is high tide, or at least, I believe it is; I hear the constant rushing of the ocean waves. Whoosh, SLAP, fizzle, sigh. Whoosh, SLAP, fizzle, sigh. I breath to its rhythm. The water pushes in and I take a breath. Away it recedes as I release the air from my heavy lungs. The damp, salty sea air is thick with the scent of mint leaves and lavender.

Stella mumbles as she smoothes something creamy and sticky over my lips; beeswax, I guess. I vaguely hear something about the roses blossoming soon. I feel a damp mint leaf being placed over my lips—her way of keeping them moist.

Even through my closed eyelids I know a cloud covers us. I don't hear any rain, but I don't feel a single ray of warmth coming through either. A breeze dances across my face. Stella must have the door open, and I enjoy the fresh air, but at times it feels as though I will never be warm. If only I could ask Stella to lay on an extra blanket. I try to form the words, but I stutter and stop, forbidden by the lack of consciousness.

"They're coming today," Stella whispers close to my face.

I'm not exactly sure how often they come—every full moon perhaps. Sometimes I think I can feel the moonlight shining above me. It always happens just after I've had a visit from my parents, the king and queen of Cray. Aunt Cornelia is always with them, along with the tonic she administers to keep me from having fits in my sleep. Often I am not able to swallow it and it runs down the side of my mouth, all the way to my chin and neck before Stella catches it with her soft cloth.

I must have mumbled something, for Stella is now murmuring, "Shhh, child. They'll be here soon. Several of the guards have already left to escort them from the boat." At least, that's what I think she said.

I wish I could see the ocean!

I remember standing on a chair in my bedroom tower and watching the thrashing waves out my window. I imagine my reflection, my baby face framed with dark golden locks, my eager expression. I can almost feel the cold stones beneath my hands as I think of it. I would lean in, pressing my face against the foggy, glazed glass, wishing I could go outside the castle more often, or that I could go on a voyage with Father as I watched his ship sail away. The memories are so fuzzy in my sleep, but some things I remember.

"There, there, Eglantine," Mother would say. "He'll return soon enough."

But it never was soon enough. I missed him every moment he was gone. Now I never see him, even when he visits. How must I look to him? Always lying still on this bed. I've done most of my growing up in my sleep. Will they even know me when I wake up? *If* I wake up.

I see her face in my mind now as the only images I recall from my fifth birthday flicker in my memory: the soft, satin silver of my dress; Aunt Cornelia's birthday gift of perfume; scores of delighted guests whose faces have grown dim over time; the giant stack of gifts I never got to open; and the witch who cursed me just after Father's toast in my honor. Two last things stand out in particular from that day all those years ago, perhaps because of how starkly they contrast one another. I can still conjure the feelings of elation that encompassed me that day, the pleasure in being the center of so much attention and celebration. And equally remembered, ringing as loud as a hundred cathedral bells in my ears, are the words of her curse. "She shall sleep forever, unless her brother frees a terrible beast."

And then, darkness. Did I fall asleep instantly? Did I sink out of my chair and onto the floor? Or was it more gradual? Did my head dip into my plate of food as I became drowsy? If only I could remember. For weeks, darkness engulfed me. And though Father moved me to the glasshouse, where fresh air and sunlight would be plentiful, most of the time I am still cumbered in darkness. I imagine I will be here always, until I grow old and pass into another world, for I have never even had a brother, and it seems I never will.

It begins to rain. I hear it pattering against the glass walls and roof of my garden dome. The rain brings an added chill, even though I am dry and covered with blankets.

"How is Eglantine today?" It's my mother's voice! I hear the shaking of parasols, but no matter how hard I try my eyes will not be pried open. I have to imagine them all. Is Mother wearing a grand dress? Or did she choose a simple one for the short sea voyage? Is her golden hair up or down? I always liked it down so that I could run my fingers through the large, soft curls. A sore ache pierces my heart whenever I think of her for the simple reason that I do not recall the color of her dainty eyes.

"Hello, Stella." And there is my father! The image of

his slender, bearded face comes to my mind. Regal with his dark hair and eyes, yet skin fair as moonlight in my memory.

Before my aunt even speaks, I know she is there, and automatically picture her auburn hair and large, deep brown eyes as she whispers in my ear. "How are you my little dumpling?" That's what she used to call me–my round, baby cheeks had reminded her of dumplings, and even as I grew and slimmed, her pet name for me lingered. I try to stir. "Lie still," she says. She sprays something into the air and the miniscule droplets of mist fall onto my face. I jerk, but do not wake. The scent is familiar. "I brought a new bottle."

She brings a new one every now and then. It is the fragrance she gave me on my fifth birthday. I used to beg her to share it with me whenever I witnessed her putting it on. It smells of dried wild roses and orange blossom. I am grateful.

Mother's lips press into my cheekbone. Her hot tears drop onto my face and run down to my ear. Perhaps she does not notice, or does not know how it tickles, even in my sleep.

"Hello, darling," she whispers.

Father kisses me also; his prickly face stirs me more than anything. He sits beside me and begins to talk, his weight rolling me toward him slightly. I think he must be reading a book, but I am becoming less aware of them all. Sleep pulls at my endlessly tired eyes, and my father's soft, deep voice only lulls me further into unconsciousness. He may as well be singing, or playing his harp for how well it sedates me.

I used to love listening to him play. Or more, loved climbing onto his lap and taking over. He would guide my arms and hands, showing me the shape and angle of my elbows, and how hard to pull at the strings. That was so long ago, another life it seems.

The memories, and the sorrow for all the happy times I've missed with them, bring a tear or two of my own. They converse amongst themselves for a time, as if I am not present. Mother complains about how pale and thin I look. Father comforts her as Stella explains how it is difficult to get me to drink my juice.

"Are you still reading to her?" Father asks.

"Yes," Stella answers.

"Every day?"

"Yes, your majesty."

I do enjoy Stella's reading, even though the words never quite seem to connect in a way that holds meaning for my lethargic mind.

It seems they just arrived, but I can sense they're preparing to go. I think it is too painful for them to see me. They must feel so helpless. Still, I wish they would stay longer. I've never seen my father cry, but though his hot tears do not fall on my face as Mother's do, he's always sniffing as he leans over me to kiss me farewell. "Goodbye, my Eggshell," he whispers. His kiss is both firm and gentle. 'Don't go,' I want to say, but my tongue is as bound as my eyes are sealed.

I hear Mother speaking softly to Stella–giving instructions, saying goodbye, or something else entirely.

"Don't cry, Redelia. For all we know, you could be carrying a child right now," Aunt Cornelia says. I imagine her comforting Mother and am grateful for an aunt to do what I cannot. Mother is not only sad for me; her barrenness disheartens her, for that prevents the spell from being broken.

My thoughts turn from them; it is too painful.

It is easier to rest, to succumb to the overpowering exhaustion, to escape to a place where I imagine there is no curse, where I may wake and run and see the earth around me.

I am only awake in my dreams.

2

BEAST

Sneaking out of the castle never proved easy, but if Prince Duncan woke precisely when the first glint of sunshine lit the sky, it was at least possible without being reprimanded. Opening his expansive chestnut wardrobe, he slid to the back and pulled down the old, slivered wooden box from the shelf. After unlocking it, he removed the tattered clothing he always wore when trying to disguise his royal identity. He slipped on the baggy white linen shirt, his right arm exposed through a large rip. Next he pulled up the shin-length wool trousers—frayed at the bottom and smelling much like perspiration and stale, dusty earth. Washing them after today would be necessary, no matter how careful he'd have to be breaking into the laundry quarters by candlelight long after it shut down for the day.

As he sauntered down the back steps, the smell of baking bread invaded his nostrils. His stomach rolled, leaving behind hunger pains and reminding him to pass by the kitchen on his way out. Looking over his shoulder, Duncan moved his bare feet across the stone floor and through an archway. He veered right, slipped down a few more steps and slowly peeked around a corner, listening for the clanging of pots and pans or Elizabeth's quick feet tapping across the floor. He crept down the remaining stairs to the entrance way of the kitchen, peering around the final corner just in time for her to come out from one of the many pantries.

Prince Duncan watched as the castle's head cook bent over her workspace (as much as a woman of her size could bend) and studied a recipe. Baskets of fruits and vegetables covered shelves that lined the walls across from her, and on the servant dining table lay seven fresh loaves of butter-topped bread, a large glass bowl filled with hard-boiled eggs, and several jars of varied fruit preserves. When Elizabeth turned and disappeared into one of the pantries, Duncan rushed forward, pulling off an end of a loaf of hot bread, ignoring the burn in his fingertips. Glancing toward her, he grabbed an egg and slipped it into his pocket, followed by an orange before he ducked out of the kitchen.

Looking both ways, he crossed a courtyard before zig-zagging through the east garden in a crouched position. Upon reaching the garden exit—an opening in the hedges where the changing guards distracted each other with talks of hunting and their families—Duncan checked back to the castle, where the tower guards walked in a large circle all hours of the day and night. When both guards had their backs to him, and the two garden guards seemed oblivious to the rest of the world outside of their trite conversation, Duncan ran for it, not catching so much as a glance from any of the guards as far as he could tell.

Once out of their sight, Duncan shoved a corner of the bread into his mouth, the salty butter greasing his lips and pleasing his taste. Elizabeth made the softest bread in all of Fallund, probably beyond. He nearly swallowed the egg whole, and then began peeling the orange as he leaned against the wall of a tailor's shop. Enough light filled the earth for shop owners along the Eastern Rows to prepare for a day of work.

Just as Duncan cut his teeth into a wedge of the sweet citrus fruit, a howl split through the quiet morning. Trying to cipher whether the sound had come from man or beast, Duncan took his dusty feet toward the cry. It was shaping up to be an adventurous day already. Howling turned to moaning, and moaning turned to screaming as Duncan neared the end of Eastern Corridor.

"Be quiet you!" ordered a man's harsh, deep voice, followed by a loud slap and whimper.

As Duncan approached, a roar of commotion

ensued. Prince Duncan quickened his shuffle, but hesitated to come around the corner boldly, so only peeked into the alley from the edge of a shop's brick wall.

Three men stood around a heap of . . . well, Duncan wasn't sure whether it was man or beast quite yet. One of them held a whip that crashed repeatedly against the pile on the ground, and the other two kicked at will. Duncan squinted, trying to recognize the form on the receiving end of all their blows. He soon determined that what looked like animal skin was actually clothing, or rags at least, much more tattered than even his current apparel. The shape turned, revealing a head of ratted hair that would cause a lion to envy.

Upon further inspection of the scene, the prince noticed one of the man's arms had a chunk the size of a good bite of bread taken out of it. Blood dripped to the ground from the wound and Duncan wondered why the idiot was beating someone rather than giving his own tear hasty medical attention.

Just then the figure on the ground leaped up onto one of the men and began biting his face.

"Pull her down," one of the men said.

Her? Could all of this fuss really be over one woman? Duncan scoffed at the idea. He rounded the corner, having finished his orange and tossed the peel. After watching the men try unsuccessfully to pry this woman off her prey, he cleared his throat in an attempt to make his presence known. When that didn't work, he finally spoke. "Gentlemen, may I be of assistance?"

"Sure, grab her there. Secure her arm," a stout, hairy man said.

"Oh, I have no intention of laying a finger on that creature. But, I am able to offer some advice. Perhaps if you stopped beating her she would prove more cooperative? Just a suggestion."

"Get out of here then, if you aren't going to help," shouted the skinny man the woman hung from as his hands forced her face away from his.

"No, really," Duncan stated. "Stop fighting her. Let her go. By order of Prince Duncan."

Two of the men paused briefly to inspect him, the other still busy with preventing facial damage.

"It is I, Prince Duncan. And I order you to let her go." He took a step forward to let them know he would intervene if they did not follow his orders.

"Your majesty, she is to be imprisoned for an awful crime. We only beat her because of her resistance."

"What crime?"

"Murder, sir."

The tall, skinny man cried out in agony as the woman sunk her teeth deep into his cheek.

"Let's grab her," Duncan said, leading the men in a final attempt to keep her from causing any one of them further harm. He tried pulling her down by one arm, and with one hand still free she slapped his eye. It stung, but that did not deter him from trying to restrain her. They each grabbed a limb after that, and with her kicking and screaming the whole way, hefted her to the prison. She forced one arm free just before entering, and held on to the iron cell door. The stout prison guard whipped her hard one last time. She let out an echoing yelp before going limp. Prince Duncan and the guards placed her on the ground and rolled her into the cell, quickly escaping any outburst or physical danger by running out and slamming the door, the key clanging in the lock soon after.

For the first time in ages, Prince Duncan noticed sweat beads forming on his forehead and arms. He marveled as he watched her. Four of them. It had taken four of them to contain her. Four of them to beat her. Four of them to calm her down with force. And he hated himself for it. For treating her that way. An overwhelming surge of pity engulfed him, but he was fascinated more than anything.

Where did she come from? What was her history that she would behave in such a way?

"Will you leave me to watch her for a while?" Duncan asked.

"Whatever you like, Prince Duncan," one of the men said. "I'll take the others for treatment if you don't mind."

"Not at all," Duncan agreed. "What is your name?"

The stout man, still holding a whip, held out his hand. "Name's Thomas. I'm head guard here. This is Phillip and Ben. Please don't be angry, Prince Duncan. We did what we had to."

The three men scurried up the steps and out onto the street. Duncan crouched down in front of the cell, gripping a cold bar in each of his hands and peering down at the figure before him. She lay about three arms lengths away, partly on her side, but both hands palm down on the dirty stone floor. Instead of a face, he saw a pile of hair that looked more like a bird's nest that had been torn apart by a predator.

Not knowing what to say, Duncan stared. An apology seemed too obvious, a question too risky. So he stayed low, watching over her in silence. He thought about her prospects had she truly murdered someone. She would be put to death by merely two statements from eye witnesses. Most murderers would hang, but some preferred to be stoned to death, which was beyond Duncan's ability to understand. He wondered which she would choose if found guilty.

She pressed on her hands and began to rise. Duncan pricked up, ready to back away if she tried to attack him through the bars. On her hands and knees now, she turned to look at him, eyes calm. Where had the woman gone from moments before, the one that would scream and bite savage chunks out of human flesh? She crawled over to the corner, slow like a wounded animal, and curled up in a ball. Only two sources of light existed in this prison, the open door and a small barred window almost directly above her. Anybody walking through the prison might not even see her in the dimness.

Suddenly feeling brave, or perhaps more curious than he could manage, Duncan spoke. "Are you all right? Is there anything that I can get for you?"

Still as the garden statues scattered about the castle grounds, seemingly breathless, she did not answer.

"Do you have a name? Do you have some family you would like me to contact?" What was he thinking? Offering such services to a peasant. No, worse than a peasant. A criminal. A murderer. Everyone he knew would scoff at such an idea. Duncan escaped the castle because of the pressures there, the decisions he didn't feel qualified to make. Ever since the king and queen had died, too many things had fallen on his shoulders, been placed in his lap, or been dragged from his head. He had had enough. But truth be told—the dirty, disgusting truth—peasants made him horribly uncomfortable, more so than those who worked in all the alleys and corridors surrounding the castle, more than he cared to admit. Those streams of business acted as a barrier, a mote keeping the rich and lush life of royalty as far as possible from the outskirts. Parents who left their children because they could not feed them, savages who fed on the raw meat of beasts if they were lucky enough to catch one, those incapable of making a living and forced to steal only to suffer a fate more cruel than hunger, all of these and more lived well beyond the comfortable world he'd known his whole life. It didn't seem fair, and a wonder swelled inside him. Why should he live a life of relative ease, constantly complaining because there were meetings to attend, wars to consider, and others struggle each day of their lives just to survive?

"Have you ever seen a court jester?" Duncan asked, feeling that if he did not find something amusing to think about soon, his heart would burst. When she didn't respond, Duncan sat down with his side against the bars, pulling his knees toward his chest and wrapping his arms around them. "I didn't think so. Well, there is this one jester, who often tries to get work inside the castle, but the only reason he ever gains admittance is because one of the maids thinks he's charming." Duncan spoke softer now, hoping to soothe, perhaps even gain her trust, and at the same time marveling that he was taking such an interest in her. "One night, before the king and queen died, a few of us in the castle let him in, telling him that this certain maid was waiting for him in the kitchen, hoping to receive a kiss from him." Duncan laughed a little, remembering well the night he and his brother had played this prank while their parents slept. "Well, we took him back to the kitchen and asked him to close his eyes. We insisted, telling him that was what she wanted. While cook was out getting some more firewood, we brought him in and toward the table, telling him to bend down low because she was short. He puckered up his lips and we guided him all the way down, where when he opened his eyes, he found the snout of a pink pig cook had just prepared for roasting the next day." Duncan couldn't control the shivers in his sides now, as he jerked about in an attempt to keep his laughter silent. Wiping the jolly tears from his eyes, he looked back to take in the sight of her, obviously unaffected, and definitely not amused, which helped him pull back his own gaiety.

Still gazing on her, he spoke again. "The king and queen were my parents. It hurts to think of them still. The pain is fresh, like a wedge of lemon sitting on the table, daring you to take a great big suck, even though it won't be very pleasant. Has anything like that ever happened to you? Anything bad?"

In the dank, dim prison, little more than a hole dug out of the ground, Duncan watched her, a mere lump in the corner, unable to see if she was even breathing. "I sure hope not. It's a terrible thing to suffer. For anyone."

Thomas returned, glaring uneasily at the girl through the bars.

Duncan couldn't bear the sight of it, the disdain this man had for her, no matter what she'd done.

Standing, Duncan faced the man as he sat down on the chair by the door. "I want you to listen to me carefully. I know that two of your men have been wounded, but given the way she was being treated, it seems to me as if it was in her own defense. Under *no* circumstances, are you to hurt her again. I want you to treat her the way you would any other prisoner, providing food and water, and clothing if she will take it. Do you understand?"

"Yes, Prince Duncan," he mumbled.

"Good. I also want you to inform me of any changes in her, whether good or bad."

"As you wish, Prince Duncan."

"Any guard who does not abide by these rules will have to answer to me, so I expect you will inform the others as soon as possible."

"Yes, Prince Duncan."

"Good." After staring him down a moment longer, Duncan returned his gaze to the woman. Crouching down once more, he spoke softly, hoping the man behind him was not listening too intently, mostly for the fact that what he was about to say seemed too personal for anyone else to hear.

"I'm going to come back. I'd like to visit you from time to time if that is all right with you. I may even come every day. Would that suit?" He hadn't been hoping for a response; he simply wanted to keep her informed. That didn't keep him from interpreting her silence to mean that she didn't protest the idea. "Good," he said. "I'm glad you don't mind."

"And one more thing. If any of the guards try to hurt you in any way again, you have my permission to defend yourself." Duncan glanced back at the guard. "*Without* any ramifications."

Taking one last look at her, allowing the pity to sink deep into his heart, Duncan vowed to himself that he would not allow this woman to suffer the fate of a murderer without trying to help her.

Finally ascending the stairs and exiting the prison, Duncan squinted under the blazing morning sun. From across the alley, a woman caught his eye, tall with dark hair. Wearing a black cloak over a floral patterned dress and hunching over slightly, she looked a bit like a witch, the kind his father had worked so hard to rid the kingdom of long ago. Her wild eyes met his, and Duncan shuffled backward, a childlike fear forcing him to abandon reason. With slow steps, she approached him, and Duncan thought it best to run away from her, but she turned, walking past him and down Northeast Alley. Paranoid, and breathing rapidly, he stared after her, not sure why she had affected him so, and although she eventually disappeared, an inexplicable panic lingered in his heart.

3

Beauty

In my dreams, I discover places and come across people. Places I have never been and people I have never met, which leaves me wondering if I created them in my head or if it is possible they are real. I suppose they are real enough to me. Most of the time, they are all I am actually aware of, for even this glasshouse in which I sleep is something I barely remember. Stella tells me it is round, though not a perfect circle, with corners and sides much like a dome I suppose, with a raised roof and vines growing all the way up it on both the inside and out. Mother and Father used it as a hot house long ago, to grow flowers in the colder months, and while space was cleared for a bed, I imagine the plants grow unhindered for I can smell them constantly. Lavender, orange blossom, and lilies so potent at times they force a sneeze from my lips, which sadly does not cause me to wake. I wonder if they grow so close to my head that Stella is constantly cutting them back, or if they surround me at a distance. Nonetheless, I feel they watch over me, as does Stella and the guards outside.

The roses grow only outdoors, but Mother will cut them and place the petals in my hand and on my cheek when they are in bloom. I am grateful, because while I can see and hear in my dreams, and sometimes I even think I can smell and taste, I cannot feel anything—not the rain on my face and arms, not the comforting embrace of my parents, not the cool, gritty sand under my feet or the wind through my hair.

As a young child (not long after falling asleep so permanently) I often dreamt of the ocean with its enormous thrashing waves, the mist swirling upward as if the water was trying to make its way back to the sky, the relentless sounds of rushing and splashing water, a gull screech now and then. But I must have grown bored of the ocean, for I began to imagine other places, places I must have learnt about or visited as a child—though I don't always remember if I did.

One haunting dream took me deep into a thick wood, something foreign to my experience, with noises that spooked and startled, noises surely belonging to unfamiliar birds and insects. And I often saw the face of the witch who cursed me, slender and filled with rage. She was in the woods that night—though it may have been day for my sleep knows no time or boundary. It was night in my dream—the moon and its reassuring light absent. As I walked, her face appeared before me.

Bodiless.

Lifeless.

Only a spirit or ghost it seemed, with gray skin, wild, course black hair, heavily wrinkled face and small, black eyes.

Paralyzed, and shaking with fear, I stopped walking, but her floating face came toward me, closer and closer, until it passed through my body and disappeared.

Only then did I hear her laugh.

I understand many would have awaken at this point in a haunting dream. I, on the other hand, kept on walking through those woods, sweating fiercely, watching over my shoulder. I feared every movement or sound, expecting her to come out from behind every tree. Panting in terror, with nobody to calm and comfort me, I raced breathlessly about that dream until Stella's cool cloth dabbed my forehead. "Shhhhh, child," she had said. "All is well." I stopped dreaming of the wood after hearing her voice and fell deeper into sleep. But I still remember, and every once in a while, the dream comes back to me, unwelcome as a spider crawling in ones bed.

I feel a yawn forming deep in my chest, and without

any warning, I am walking the halls of a grand castle. At first I am delighted, thinking I must be paying a visit home, which after all these years is still my heart's first desire. Exuberance fills me up as I turn around, trying to remember which way it is to my room, or Father's study, or Mother's reading room, or the kitchen for a bite of salty ham. But I am lost. I do not know this castle. Disheartened at the realization, I amble about, opening doors to peek inside until I learn that I can actually walk through them. Still hoping to happen upon a kitchen as I long for a bite of real food (even if imaginary) I keep at it until I enter a room where a man sits in a dull, wooden chair. The fingers of his right hand drum rhythmically on a table fit for dozens as he bows his head toward a stack of unrolled parchment. I want to get a look at his face so I move closer, thinking that if I bend down I might find success, but he is too enthralled with the words before him.

He shuffles the papers, which startles me and I am for some reason all together afraid of being caught nosing around. Mother used to get after me for that. I try to calm down, realizing I am only in a dream, unobtrusive, even invisible to him. I open my lungs to a long, deep breath and push the air out slowly. A solitary sheet of parchment on the table below me flutters slightly, as if my breath had affected it. Impossible. So I blow again, this time harder, as if I intend to blow out the nineteen candles that will be on my next birthday cake, and every loose sheet of parchment quivers under the force.

The man slaps his hands on top of them, attempting to keep them from flying off the table. Amused, I blow again.

Exasperated, he speaks. "What– What is going on?" And then he looks up, his face finally visible, his eyes resting exactly on mine, or so it seems. "How did you get in here?"

I hadn't been expecting this.

It is rare that I actually interact with someone in my dream, and in all honesty, I'm not in the mood for it right now. The people in my dreams never answer my questions correctly, and often nothing they say makes any sense. And so I just stare, studying his square jaw and strong, pleasant face. I wonder why it is that he shaves so closely, and if tunics with vests are still the fashion or if it is only because I am dreaming that he wears similar clothing to what Father's young court members used to wear.

"Are you deaf?" he asks, and I can't think why on earth he would ask such a question. There is nothing whatsoever wrong with my hearing, unless you count the fact that I am in and out of varying levels of consciousness all the time.

His eyebrows come together above his dark hazel eyes. I assume it is a visible sign that he thinks me a puzzle to figure out.

But why had my breath sent his papers flying? I blow again, this time to no avail. Not a trifle of disturbance among the papers on the table.

"What on earth are you doing?" he asks.

"I'm dreaming. What on earth are *you* doing?" He is the most unpleasant person I have ever dreamt of.

"Don't be absurd. You're awake as I am. I can see plainly for myself." He stands up in front of me, placing his hands on the table before him. "How did you get in here? Who are you? What is it you want?"

How do I answer? I begin to grow hot now, feeling the depth of his irritation, my insecurities about nosing around surfacing once more. But I am dreaming. None of it is real. Perhaps it is time for a little fun as I rarely have such an opportunity in my dreams to irritate someone.

"I came in through the wall. Isn't that how all people enter rooms? My name is Eglantine, princess of Cray, and all I want is a little refuge from the dullness of my existence. Forgive me for thinking I could find that here with you." I begin to approach the door, excited about the prospect of leaving this man and hopefully even the memory of him behind. I wonder if finding the kitchen is still a possibility before this dream vanishes from me.

"Wait a minute. Did you say you are a princess? From Cray?"

"Why yes, I did. You have extremely excellent hearing for one so impossible." I take a few more steps toward the door before he speaks again.

"I'm sorry," he says. "I didn't realize without the proper introduction. Did Duke show you in? Did your father send you?"

"Father? Why would Father send me? I haven't seen Father in nearly fifteen years. And how is it that I can converse so easily with you?"

I watch his face, a mystified far-off look in his eyes. He must be working it out on his own since my answers cannot satisfy him. Finally a look of recognition spreads over his brow, calming the wrinkles, settling the confusion.

"You're the princess? Of Cray?"

"Yes," I answer.

"The sleeping princess?" He is pointing at me now with a finger from his right hand.

"How did you know?"

I stare at him a moment longer. Who is he? What is actually happening inside this dream? I don't like his eyes so intently focused on me, blazing into my own eyes it seems.

"I used to know you when we were children," he admits.

A bustle of bodies and commotion bursts through the door.

"You'll have to excuse me," he says. "We have a meeting. Duke will show you down to the entry room where you may wait for me. I'd be happy to speak with you after our meeting."

"No, wait," I protest. "Are you actually a person? Can you really see me? And hear me?"

"Yes, of course I can. I'm not an invalid."

The men begin taking their seats around the table. A plump, curly-haired maid pushes a cart and begins to set tea cups in front of them. Steam rises from a teapot and the clanking and filling up of cups alerts me to the fact that I do not belong here.

"Who are you speaking with, Prince Henry?" the stout man beside him asks.

I've been talking to a prince. He didn't act very much like a prince. He holds out his hand toward me, answering the question with a nod of the head in my direction.

The man looks over to me, near my shoulder, about my hip, finally settling his eyes to the side of me, where on the wall just behind hangs an oil painting of the sea. The green and blue do not blend well, but crash into one another. It is noisy, like the ocean. Never once did he look me straight in the eyes. I have never in my life felt more like a tiny insect than I do in this moment. I may as well be a fly on the wall, or the moth flitting about the window, or the spider spinning its web in the corner of the floor where nobody would notice. I feel swallowed up by a sense of loneliness, nothing but a dreamer, a spectator to events that don't exist, an inventor of people and places.

"I do not see anyone in the room besides the men who entered with me, and you were having a conversation before we entered. Who was it you were talking to?"

"It was her, I tell you," he said. I feel grateful that he is no longer irritated with me, or at least if he is, I am not the one he is yelling at.

All of the men exchange glances now, not understanding the prince means me, who they cannot see.

"Did you get much sleep last night?" One of the men asks. His greatest feature is his large, pointed nose. "There is no one in the room but those of us sitting at this table and your maid."

"Oh, how can you be so impossible?" the prince asks. "Now is not the time for playing pranks."

"Ask your maid then," the stout man says. "She will have no reason to prank you, and her job would be on the line if she did."

"Oh, fine. Marie, do you see a young woman standing before the sea painting?"

She looks in my direction, her eyes closer to the mark than any of them, but I know instantly that she too cannot see me.

"No, your majesty." She immediately continues her work, setting places for others they must be expecting.

"But *you* can see me?" I ask, a strange, hopeful sort of nervousness arousing inside of me, as well as a longing to stay here. If only he can really see me, I want nothing more than to stay. He does not answer, but he does not need to. His dark hazel eyes stare directly into mine. After clearing his throat and looking away from me, he sits down.

"Let's get started, shall we?" he says.

"Oughtn't we to wait for Prince Duncan?" I do not know who said it exactly, someone to my right. I cannot take my eyes off of him–Prince Henry if that is his name. I do not ever want to take my eyes off of him. He can see me!

"Can you hear me as well?" I ask.

He pauses for a moment, halting the pen in his hand which had previously been scratching something on the parchment in front of him. He keeps from glancing up at me, but I know he heard.

"Is something wrong, Prince Henry?" Again, I don't know who said it. I keep my eyes locked on his nut-brown hair, lying straight on top of his head, cut short, spreading in two directions from an off-centered part. The door opens. The maid steps out, taking the noise of the cart with her.

"Henry?" another asks.

"We do not need to wait for Duncan," he replies.

I don't mind that he chose not to answer my question. I know my dream could end at any moment, so I persist, walking around the table and to the side of Henry. Prince or not, he can see me. I know he can. And if he thinks to ignore me, I plan to make that difficult for him, maybe even impossible. Now that I think of it, I should have just walked through the table and sat down on top of all the parchment. I'll try being tactful first.

"Okay, let's get started," the stout man says.

"What is your meeting about?" I ask the prince, leaning in close to him from behind.

He jumps back.

I must have startled him.

"Is something the matter?" one of the men asks. There are only three of them besides the prince: the stout one next to him, pointed nose closest to the door, and a man with nearly perfect posture across from Henry. It appears there is actually a stick in his back keeping any curving over at bay. He is the one who had spoken.

"No, of course not," Henry said.

"Are you sure?" I ask, plopping in the chair on his free side.

He grits his teeth. Impressed with how still and collected he seems, I watch his face redden. His eyes meet mine, and they hold a warning of sorts.

"I'm sorry," I say. "Is there something you would like to say to me?"

"Get. Out." It comes softly, but clearly.

"Out of what?" I ask. "The chair? Oh, sorry."

"Prince Henry, are you sure everything is satisfactory? Shall I call the maid for more tea?" the man with the pointed nose inquires.

"No," the prince says. "Charles, please continue." Prince Henry rubs his forehead and I almost feel poorly for behaving so cruelly. Almost, but not quite.

"Shall I call the maid for *hotter* tea? Is it hotter tea you need?" I ask him. "Or a doctor perhaps? Are you feeling unwell?"

"That's it," he says, slamming his quill onto the table and rising to his feet. He stomps to the door and exits the room. Naturally, I follow.

"What on earth are you trying to do? Make a fool of me?"

"No, of course not."

"Then why are you acting that way?"

"Because I've never met anyone who could see me before."

He stands there facing me, and for a moment I think I can feel his hot breath on my face. Perhaps I am mistaken, but there is no mistaking that he can hear me or see me, which gives me an idea. I reach out my hand toward him, all my fingers pointing at his chest. Wondering if I will be able to feel it beneath my fingertips in only a moment, I breath in deep, a distant crashing of waves sounding beyond the two of us.

And Stella's voice. I can hear Stella. I force my hand to close the remaining distance but it is no use.

I cannot feel him.

"What are you doing?" he asks.

I don't understand. Why is it that he can see me and hear me when the others can't? Why does he seem so real? I study my hand, disappointed that it was unable to do what I wanted. Ashamed, I cannot look at him. Stella's voice grows louder. The ocean calls me back home.

4

BEAST

Duncan jolted awake, breathless and drenched in sweat. A sense of peril still gripped him, a fear for his life, and he wanted to run–run so far away that she could never haunt his dreams again. He attempted to get some visual in the darkness, groping for anything familiar. Disoriented, he searched his thoughts. Had he fallen asleep in his own bed or one of the many extra bedrooms throughout the castle? Which part of the grounds would be outside the window? The statue of his mother and father? The hedge rows that created geometrical shapes if you looked down at them from the second or third floor? Feeling the linen sheets beneath him that covered a soft, down feather mattress, and the wool blanket surrounding his legs and chest, he eased only slightly, finally becoming aware of an angry thirst brought on by a parched mouth and lips so void of moisture they burned. He reached blindly for the goblet resting on his bedside table and brought it to his lips, tilting it up over his mouth, waiting for the relief that wouldn't come. Not even a single drop remained. After attempting to place the goblet back in its spot only to drop it onto the floor, Duncan pulled on the string that would ring for a servant.

She'd been haunting his dreams for days now, the old woman he'd seen outside the prison's open stone entrance, the woman looking at him expectantly, as if she'd been waiting for him. Though they hadn't spoken, Duncan felt as if she had entered his thoughts, searched his soul, begged his help, and condemned him all in one solitary encounter, all with one piercing stare. Now her face was all he could see.

A creak sounded and the prince looked for his servant.

"What is it, Master Duncan?"

"Water. Karl, will you please bring me a drink of water?"

Throwing his head back onto the pillows, Duncan waited until he returned. He must have fallen asleep, because he jolted as he heard the sound of a new goblet being set on the bedside table.

"Thank you, Karl."

The servant left, dragging his tired feet as Duncan seized the goblet and practically threw the water down his throat, spilling onto his face, shirt and bedding.

Taking deep breaths, Duncan tried to force the memory of the old woman's face from his head. He thought of the summer meadows in the Westlands, the wildflowers showing their brilliant purples, blues and yellows, the sun burning down on his head, his brother running along side him with their father lagging behind and their mother yelling "don't be too long!" It had been their yearly excursion to escape the pressures of palace life, and Duncan cherished the memories, acting as a bright, warm light whenever things seemed cold and dark.

Though the hold she'd seemed to have on him during the dream had faded, there, behind her withering image, was the prison girl–neither human nor beast in entirety, but a combination of the two. Duncan began thinking of her there in the cold dark corner. Did she even know how to speak? All of the yelling guards in the world would have made no difference if she had no understanding of language. Then a word came to mind–one he'd thought of over and over the last few days, circling around and around like an endless whirlpool. Murder.

This growing obsession would not rest, this fascination for someone he did not know, someone he wasn't even sure he wanted to know–a peasant in peasant clothing, a beast in human skin.

If he did nothing, the restlessness would surely drive him crazy. Duncan threw off his covers and pulled the servant bell again. Following a warm bath and an hour or so of preparation before the sun crept into view (waking everyone else in the castle) Duncan would locate Henry—the brother he'd spoken to so little since the king and queen had died, the twin who surely hated him for neglecting every responsibility, dodging every council and avoiding any conversation. Worried he'd left his brother feeling abandoned, and not comfortable with the prospects or ramifications of that, Duncan felt increasingly uncomfortable in his presence. But it couldn't be helped. Duncan hated it—all of it—the nobility, the stuffiness of royal ways, the countless hours making decisions that didn't seem to make any difference, the expectations, and while it consoled him that he at least felt sick about it at times, he would not be forcing himself to do things he hated. Life as a prince had deprived him of so many other freedoms, this one he would not give up. Their father had always intended for Henry to rule and Duncan to smile and shake hands. And whenever he came in contact with anyone, whether in the castle or out, that is exactly what he did.

The door opened.

The raspy voice of Karl sounded again, an insult to

the quiet morning. "You rang...again...Master Duncan." Karl had to be older than the kingdom itself, and while his slow speech often held long pauses, Duncan knew this had been exaggerated, his way of letting the prince know he didn't enjoy being woken up before the split of dawn.

Not like he could murmur. Duncan rarely asked him for anything, and could boast being the most self-sufficient royalty in at least three generations.

"Thank you for coming, Karl. Will you please prepare water for a bath and iron some fresh clothing?"

"If Master Duncan plans on leaving the castle unattended...again...I recommend a disguise. Would you like me to iron a dress?"

"Your humor is impeccable Karl, especially for so early in the morning. I congratulate you. Perhaps you're right. Forget the ironing, I'll wear my usual attire."

Duncan cringed at the thought, having never taken his peasant clothing to be laundered as intended, but rather stuffed the garments back in the box where he usually kept them.

"Quite, Master Duncan. I am always right." He turned to leave but before he'd gone too far, Duncan called, "Karl, where will Prince Henry be this morning?"

Karl deliberated momentarily. "Let's see, being the

middle of the week, he will most likely be found on the grass outside bowling, or perhaps taking a stroll through one of the gardens." He'd averted eye contact during the whole act, looking all around him and above, but never directly at his master. Duncan withheld a response, not entirely sure of his meaning.

"He'll be in the council chambers within the hour, sire. He rarely leaves, except for an afternoon excursion to inspect the various sectors of the castle from time to time."

"I see," Duncan said. Karl had meant to insult him, to imply that had Duncan paid more attention or worked as he should, he would know exactly where to find his brother. He stood tall, not letting the sarcasm get to him. "Thank you, Karl."

Karl left and Duncan entered his wardrobe, pulling down the box where he kept his smelly peasant clothing. Perhaps he should have had Karl bring something ironed after all (despite his stinging remarks and maybe because of them) so at least he would look respectable when facing his brother. An old, familiar insecurity rushed through him. Duncan took a moment to finger through the garments hanging in his wardrobe–white shirts with sleeves that puffed out far too much for his taste and strapped around the waste to a single button on the back side, hosen and breeches, and leather shoes he never wore.

Duncan placed his hands on the back wall of the wardrobe and leaned forward, placing his head against the smooth, cold wood. How long he stood there, debating what direction his life should take (or would take if he kept on this way) he did not know.

Startled by the sound of Karl behind him announcing that a warm bath awaited, Duncan grabbed a clean shirt and an old pair of breeches he planned to tear near the shins. He would go barefoot. Even if he smelled fresh and wore clean clothes, he knew people really judged station in life by the shoes one wore. He could stand in confidence before his brother with a clean shirt, and pass for a peasant once outside the castle grounds because of his dirty feet.

"Will there be anything else?" Karl asked.

"No. You've been most helpful. Thank you Karl, especially for coming so early and with such short notice."

"You're welcome, Master Duncan."

After a bath Duncan couldn't believe Karl had described as warm, the prince dressed and ran his fingers through his hair. He knew Henry couldn't stand a hairy face, but couldn't remember the last time he'd seen a shaving knife. Perhaps he'd visit a barber today, but probably not.

Duncan stopped by the kitchen for a quick bite of toast and jam. Elizabeth begrudgingly gave him an orange as well, knowing they were his favorite, snorting her disapproval and turning up her nose. Even the cooks despised him for breaking tradition and not eating at the royal breakfast table.

"Thank you Elizabeth," Duncan said, smiling sincerely.

Just as Karl had predicted, Henry sat at the table in the council chambers, a stack of leather bound books before him and a parchment immediately under his nose. He looked up as Duncan entered, but returned to his scribbling.

"You're up early," Henry said.

"So are you," Duncan replied.

"I'm always up this early," Henry scoffed.

"So am I," Duncan answered.

Henry scribbled away. "Did you come here to say anything important? I have work to do."

Duncan found himself tongue tied. Why had he come again? Oh, yes. The girl. He opened his mouth only to be cut off before he formed a sentence.

"Where have you been lately? Nobody seems to be able to find you. Ever."

Duncan sighed. He hated interrogation. "Oh, around."

Henry chuckled darkly. "Not around here." He stopped writing and looked at his brother. Duncan braced himself. He knew that look; a scolding soon followed. "You know, you should be more careful. Gallivanting around the rows and alleys and who knows where else is a good way to get mauled."

Had he heard about the girl? The beast in prison for murder? Duncan hadn't actually been mauled, but he could have been.

"I have a good mind to start sending Worston after you as punishment."

"Not Worston," Duncan murmured. "He's the worst."

"Yes, he remembers well our growing up years and the soap you used to slip into his tea."

"Well why doesn't he hate you then? I wasn't the only one slipping things into his tea."

"*I* apologized." Henry held his head high for a moment, arrogant and condescending.

"Do as you wish, Brother." Duncan turned to leave. He should never have come. Talking to Henry could be so objectionable. It was no wonder Duncan worked so hard to avoid him.

Just as Duncan reached for the door, Henry's grating voice sounded again.

"Duncan, what do you know of the sleeping princess?"

Looking over his shoulder Duncan answered, "She's asleep." He hadn't intended to stop, but Henry stood and continued to quiz him.

"Yes, but what else?"

Duncan listed what he knew. "She was cursed as a child. Her father blamed our kingdom and stopped all trade."

"Yes, I know all that. But what else?"

"I know nothing else."

Prince Henry hesitated for a moment. "But she's not dead, right? She wouldn't be a ghost?"

"I haven't heard of anything like that. Why? Have you?"

"No, of course not," Henry answered.

"Why are you suddenly so interested in the sleeping princess?"

Henry reached an arm up and grabbed a section of his own hair, looking frazzled, perhaps even frustrated that Duncan provided nothing significant.

"Never mind. It's nothing." Henry stood there, thinking about something and Duncan longed for the days of not so long ago, when they'd shared everything.

Now was his chance. If he was ever going to ask his brother for help, or for information at least, it had to be right now, right after his brother had sought knowledge from him, even if he'd had nothing to give.

Turning away from the door, Duncan asked, "Henry, do you know anything about the woman in prison?"

Duncan watched his brother's face. He looked as though his thoughts had shattered and he'd been brought back to reality. Then he pulled a look of confusion, the same face he'd seen on his brother countless times, like whenever their father had told a joke.

"Why do you want to know?"

Duncan knew being direct would produce the best results. "I want to help her if I can."

"Well, I heard she is wild—something of a creature rather than man. Perhaps she's a barbarian. They do slip into our borders from time to time."

Prince Duncan thought about that. The barbarians lived to the south and west of them, acting as a barrier of sorts, separating them from the unfriendly country of Tern.

"And she'll be tried for murder, eventually. There is

only one witness, but we can't afford to hold prisoners endlessly. She will be tried and the court will decide."

"When?"

Henry sat back down and reached into the piles of books, pulling down the second from the top. He opened it up, flipping toward the back. He turned them one by one now, until at last he found what he'd been searching for. Looking up at his brother he revealed what he'd found. "Fourteen days to allow for another witness, after that, who knows. It may depend on whether we need the prison cell. We can't keep anyone else in there with her."

"What if another witness doesn't come forward? What will happen to her then?"

"It depends on the outcome of the court hearing. If she isn't found guilty, which is doubtful given her conduct, she will be banished at the very least."

"Thank you, Brother." He turned to leave again.

"We'd love to see you at the next council meeting." Henry sounded annoyed more than hopeful, more humored than serious.

"I'll do what I can." Duncan waved but Henry called him back.

"Oh, and Duncan?"

"Yes?"

"I'm sure Karl would take a nice sharp knife to your face if you asked nicely."

"He might."

"Oh, and Duncan?"

"Yes?"

"Find some shoes." A smile Henry attempted to suppress crept up on his mouth.

Duncan rolled his eyes, calling, "No promises" over his shoulder as he left, heading toward the closest rear exit and hoping Henry hadn't been serious when he'd threatened to send Worston after him.

Low, thin rain clouds blocked much of the sun's light, and a sort of mist filled the air, as if the rain came from a source other than the sky.

Hurrying through the stone paths of the garden and onto the muddy roads, Duncan headed straight for Northeast Alley. The slight rain did not deter local merchants from opening their shops.

A guard stood at the top prison step, inspecting the gray sky. "Looks like it may not last long," he said as Duncan got closer.

"Quite," Duncan agreed. "How's the girl today?"

The guard looked at him. "Why, Prince Duncan, we hadn't expected you back."

"Well, for now, don't be surprised to see me. I will be visiting the woman regularly, and I want you to keep me informed if anything changes with her trial or with the witness."

"Yes, your majesty."

"May I see her?"

He turned around, the ring of keys attached to his side by a rope clanging with the movement. "Of course, sire. Follow me."

The rain had dampened all the stone steps and a portion of the dirt floor. Darker and damper than usual, the prison brought a dreary feeling to Duncan, a feeling of hopelessness and surrender, of doom and foreboding, of insecurity about where he stood and why he'd come. Could coming here make any difference in the world to her? Could anything be done?

Seeing her there, a little way off from the corner and the mist coming through the window, still curled as if asleep or in great pain, Duncan gathered a little courage.

"Does she take any nourishment?" Duncan asked.

"Only water, sire. We haven't been able to get her to eat anything."

Duncan considered the conversation with his brother, his mentioning of the barbarians. "What's your name?" he asked the guard.

"Phillip, sire."

Duncan offered his hand, and as they shook, he noticed a bandage wrapped tightly around the man's arm from the wounds she'd inflicted in their attempts to imprison her. "Phillip, what have you tried giving her to eat?"

"Oh, all kinds of things, sire. Bread, fish, fruits and vegetables. Thomas even brought a bit of stew from home once. She wouldn't touch it."

Could it be? Could she really be a barbarian, a member of a cruel and blood thirsty people? And why then, would she be accused of murder? Barbarians killed anyone who crossed into their imagined borders.

"Phillip," Duncan said. "I want you to try raw meat."

"Raw meat, sire?" he asked, looking sideways at the prince as they stood before the prison cell.

"Yes, Phillip. Raw meat."

5

Beauty

Stella read to me once a story about a man who could never fall asleep. I wonder what it must be like for a person to live with such a dilemma. They must stare at their ceilings, out their windows, too many thoughts circling about in their minds, all the while sleep eluding them. It is the opposite for me. I long to be awake, to walk along the beach and place my hands in the cool ocean water, to feel the waves crash upon my legs and try to take me with them, to lie in my bed at night, restless and wide awake, or perhaps even tired. What would it feel like to be tired but unable to sleep?

I remember as a child sitting near the fireplace in my father's study. As he read a book with his glasses resting on the tip of his nose, wrote a letter with the quill scratching on the parchment, or just rested his eyes as a minstrel sang an epic poem, I could feel my eyelids growing so heavy, and my muscles seemed to melt before Stella could persuade me to my bed. She would carry me in her arms when at last

I'd fallen asleep on the floor. Nothing could wake me then, just as nothing can wake me now.

While some lie awake, wishing that sleep would come and take them away, I lie asleep, wishing more than anything to open my eyes and wake up to the world around me.

I ache for movement, and in an attempt to get some exercise, I will often find myself running through an open field, or even flying above the buildings of the kingdom in an exerting dream, only to be swallowed up by the rising ocean waves. Drowning must feel a little like the spell I'm under.

I vaguely hear the harmonic chirping of crickets, a signal that it is most likely night time. I remember listening to them outside the castle walls when Father and Mother would let me stay up late and run through the garden trying to catch fire flies.

"Why do they make that sound?" I asked Father once.

"It is their station to make music for the night sky," Father answered. "Just as the moon exists to give us light in the darkness, crickets live to fill the silence with music."

I love listening to their song, but I do not wish to stay here in this glasshouse with Stella. Ever since meeting

Prince Henry, I have longed to find him again. I want to know if he can really see and hear me, or if it was only a cruel trick of my slumbering state. If I were to find him, would I be able to talk with him as I had before? And how do I find him?

Rarely am I able to control what I dream about. I will begin to think about a pleasant place or memory, and then drift further and deeper into rest. At times, the dream is worth remembering, but there are also times when the dream will take a bizarre turn. The meadow I want to run through will grow vines that trip my feet; the roses of the rose garden will be dying and there is nothing I can do to save them; or someone I love, like Father or Mother or Aunt Cornelia, will try to harm me. Even in dreams you cannot escape the reality that life is full of both the extraordinary and the dull, both the elating and the sorrowful, the calm and the dangerous. All things, especially good dreams, are terminable, but that does not mean they are incapable of leaving a permanent impression.

If I had truly met Prince Henry, and he could actually see and hear me, couldn't that mean that I had experienced a bit of real life in my dream? That though danger and sadness are part of the natural order, if I was with him in reality, and not merely in a state of dreaming, I would only be subject to *real* danger and sadness, and not the torment of a strangely horrible dream that would not loosen its grasp on me?

I want to know.

I *need* to find him again.

Accepting that if I do find him things may or may not be like they were before, I decide to try. The prospect of finding him only to learn that he was like any other person in my dreams—intangible and unintelligent—and that he could not converse with me, rustles my thoughts at first, causing little butterflies of insecurity to flit about my stomach and around my heart. I banish the idea and focus solely on the kingdom of Fallund, its grassy hillsides and spacious meadows, its wheat fields and forests, its tiny bit of ocean front with majestic cliffs, and its dark, circular castle, topped with a single tower.

We had visited Fallund once in my short childhood, and I could remember well the sites we frequented, and the landscapes we had traveled through. It was impractical to go by ship, the country being for the most part land-locked, bordered on the north by my own kingdom of Cray, and on the south and west by Tern.

I imagine a carriage, black and round, complete with two white horses and a driver. The horses neigh and whine as the wind blows their wild manes about. The driver is dark as well, hooded and cloaked in a robe of black, but I can see his face, and though a little blurry and indistinguishable, it does not appear unkind. Lastly, I create in my dream a beautiful gown, scarlet and jeweled, covered by a dark brown kirtle, and wear my hair in a braided bun. The sky above, not vast as normal, but only directly above the carriage and me, looks like it will send rain.

"Where would you like to go?" the driver asks, and he sounds much older than he appears.

"To Fallund," I yell above the wind. Has he heard me? My voice seems to catch on a piece of breeze and float away.

He looks ahead of him, muttering something to the horses. "Get in then," he yells back.

I board the carriage in two quick steps. There are no doors, and thankfully, no other passengers. It is night, and a dark one at that, so I cannot see where we are going, or what the scenery looks like. Nothing but black passes by, so I lean my head back and rest, closing my eyes and drawing in deep, lengthy breaths.

When the carriage rumbles and jolts to a stop, I open my eyes and sit up.

"This is as far as I go," the man yells back to me.

"They don't let carriages on castle grounds."

Castle grounds? I lean outside the carriage and there it is, the circular castle with a single tower, only the tower raises all the way up into the sky that is still only big enough to cover the things immediately around me. Light blazes from behind every window.

I step down from the carriage, and as I look back to see one of the horses watching me, they all vanish. Only the castle and I exist now, separated by a grand, seemingly eternal expanse of hedge rows.

Looking to the ground I see that a dirt path will lead me into the hedges and up to the castle door. I set one foot, covered in a silver jeweled shoe, onto the path. After turning two corners it becomes clear that making my way to the castle will not be easy. The hedges form a maze, and while they are low enough to see over, I still cannot make out a designated pathway. I lift up my dress, surprised at how light it is, and begin stepping over the hedges with great ease. Delighted by this ability, I begin leaping until my eagerness takes over and I soar into the sky, taking care to stay high enough to avoid crashing with the hedges, and low enough that I should land easily in front of the castle. I am a bit wobbly, teetering from side to side, and as I fly, the rows of hedges multiply so the castle grows distant again.

Frustrated, I pull myself down out of the sky and onto the ground, landing again amid the hedges.

Then I hear voices.

"Hello, Prince Duncan."

"Hello, Worston."

I walk over the hedges again until the castle door finally comes into view. Two bright flames light the front of the castle and part of the grounds. Looking up, I see the stars, the sky now its normal size and appearance. Not a cloud in sight, the partial moon shines bright above me as well, and the air is perfectly still. I wonder about the driver for a moment. Had he ever really been? Or was he only a creation of my mind? Will I ever see him again?

Footsteps sound on the stone ground surrounding the castle, and a man comes into view. I stand in front of the castle door so I will be in his way. At first I think it's Henry, but upon further inspection I realize his face is to bristly, more like Father's. And his hair is too long. But whoever he is, I hope he can see me anyway. He walks with sure, steady steps up to the door and knocks. Another man answers through a small window, his voice muffled. "Who is it?"

The man standing right next to me, practically right in front of me, yells back. "It's Prince Duncan." His loud voice shakes and rattles me, piercing my ear like an unexpected crack of thunder in the sky.

The door opens. "Prince Duncan, you know you're not supposed to be out so late."

"My apologies."

"Your brother has been asking for you. He would like you to come to council tonight."

"Thank you for the message," the prince says, smiling warmly as he steps inside and down a corridor. I don't remember much about the royal family of Fallund, and briefly wonder how many princes or princesses there might be. It seems already the king and queen of Fallund are more blessed than my own dear parents.

The door slides shut in front of me. I had missed my chance. I place my hand on the door, hoping I will pass through anyway, but to no avail.

More footsteps approach and a man walks right up to the door and shouts, "It's Worston, let me in."

The door opens and I steal my chance, slipping inside simultaneously.

Instantly I am carried away to an upper level of the castle tower. Looking around, I determine that I have made it. A balcony opens up to a foyer below graced by a statue of what I assume is the royal family of Fallund. As I turn around, I realize I am standing in the exact place where I had last conversed with Henry, outside his council room. Clearing my throat, I raise my hand to knock and as I do it falls through the door and I step inside effortlessly.

There he sits, in the exact chair, studying what could even be the same parchments for all I know. Dark half moons below his eyes tell me he's had little sleep lately. I think of how lucky he is, to be able to work late and rise early, or to toss and turn for lack of rest. Then he lay his head in his hands, a deep, heavy sigh escaping from his mouth. What could be troubling him so? Hesitating, I smooth the fabric of my dress. It looks so much brighter than it had when I'd first boarded the carriage in the darkness. And now here I am, having reached my destination and I am too afraid to open my mouth.

I clear my throat, never expecting that such a simple gesture of preparation could cause such a stir. Prince Henry jumps up, forcing his seat back ever so slightly.

"How did you get in here?" he asks. Then those dark hazel eyes narrow in on me. "It's you," he says.

Relief sweeps over me. He remembers! And he can still see me. One final test remains.

"Hello, Prince Henry. It's nice to see you again."

"Nice? I wouldn't describe our last encounter as nice.

You disturbed me before an important briefing and made me look like a fool in front of my closest councilman and aides. And you're wearing your nightgown again." He nods at me, raising a finger to point. "If you'd like to have an audience with me, you will have to wear appropriate attire."

My mouth drops open.

Mortified, I look down to see one of the white nightgowns Stella dresses me in. Where is my scarlet dress? My brown kirtle? I reach up to touch my hair, hoping desperately that the braid and bun held fast. Alas, my golden hair reaches down long past my shoulders, probably wind swept from my journey. I look behind me hoping to find a mirror, but there is only the painting of the sea.

"Like I said," the prince begins, picking up a quill and scratching away on the parchment before him. "Proper dress next time please. Oh, and make an appointment. Now if you'll excuse me." His focus has completely switched, from his surprise at first seeing me, to his love for insults, to whatever business he's conducting on that parchment.

But I have come all this way, in a dream mind you, hoping for some human connection. I would have preferred polite conversation, but he can hear me, so I easily look past his negativity.

"What is it you're working on?"

Prince Henry continues to write, never breaking except to dip his quill in ink. His lips move as he writes, as if he carries on a conversation with himself, or perhaps he's merely mouthing the words in whatever correspondence he's working on.

The door opens and in steps a short, thin, elderly man with white hair pulled back in a ponytail. "Your majesty, it is time for the council. The men will be arriving shortly."

"Thank you, Duke." Prince Henry finally puts his quill down and stands up. "Tell Marie to bring plenty of refreshments. I expect the meeting will go on for quite some time."

"Yes, your majesty." The elderly man pulls the door closed, leaving us alone once again.

The prince turns to me. His hair looks a little darker today, perhaps because of the dim lighting. "Look, I need you to leave."

"But I just got here." It took such great effort to find him again, and I have no intention of leaving.

"I don't know what you are, but you are not welcome here. So if you are a ghost or a fairy or some hallucination, I still need you to leave." His eyebrows drawn together, he glares at me. "I'm sorry," he says finally, but I know he isn't. It's only a formality. There isn't a hint of regret in those stern eyes.

"So am I," I reply. "Because I am not leaving. You said before that we knew each other as children? I don't remember."

The door bursts open and a flood of men come through, including the three I recognize from our previous encounter. They are followed by Marie and her tray of delicious looking food—cakes and breads and jams the rich colors of red and purple—and Duke. Standing tall, Duke announces the start of the meeting once all the men are seated. "Is there anything else you will be needing from me?" Duke asks.

"Only Prince Duncan if you can find him," Henry replies. "Thank you, Duke."

He bows his head as he pulls back on the door and exits.

The prince takes in the sight of all the men surrounding him who look back expectantly. He glances at me as though he's unsure of what to do.

"Don't let me keep you from your important meeting," I say.

The prince clears his throat and quickly looks away from me. "Let's see, I have called you all here tonight..."

I sit down in front of him, right between two serious

looking men. I turn to the man on my right and say, "Excuse me, would you have a cigar I could borrow? These meetings always drag on and I like to stay relaxed."

Prince Henry glares at me.

"What is it your majesty?" one of the men asks. It is one of the men from before, the one with the big, pointy nose. "Why have you called us here tonight?"

"I have called you here tonight..."

"How's your family?" I ask the man to my left. "Oh, pardon me, but you have a flake on your nose. Let me get that for you." I reach my tiniest finger and pretend to flick some imaginary speck from his nose.

I glance at the prince, smiling at my victorious attempts to get on his nerves. He glares back at me.

"I have asked all of you to come here tonight because..."

"Excuse me, your candle is dripping wax all over the desk and Prince Henry really hates that," I say to a man across the table and down a ways.

"Enough!" the prince yells.

"Enough of what?" I ask.

Several of the men whisper to each other, but I do not hear what they say.

"Stop this at once." It is softer than his previous

outburst, but not less threatening.

"Who is it you're talking to?" the man seated to my right asks. "Have we done something to offend you?"

He doesn't look at me, but I know I am the recipient of his next remarks. "Look, if you would like to wait outside, I would be happy to talk to you after the council meeting."

The men whisper again, almost all of them, covering their mouths and glancing at the prince, their ruler and leader.

"I don't want to wait outside."

"Why not?"

"Because I'm afraid."

"What on earth are you afraid of? Duke is probably the only one right outside that door and he's so loving he won't even step on insects."

"Prince Henry, what is this all about?"

I speak up quickly, so that Henry pays attention to me rather than the man questioning him. "I'm afraid that if I walk out that door, I will lose contact with you." How desperate that must sound! Why would I even matter to him? I brave further explanation. "You're the only one who can hear me. The only one I have to talk to."

He clears his throat once more and shifts in his seat,

as though my words have caused him discomfort.

He looks me in the eye, not glaring or condemning, just searching for something. "You may stay. But please let me finish my meeting."

I nod, grateful for the risk he took in speaking to me in front of all these men who respect him and look to him for guidance.

A heavy sigh escapes him once more. "Men, I have called you here tonight to let you know we are at war." He pulls an envelope from his vest pocket and places it on the table. "I'll let you read it yourselves. Conner, please inform Prince Duncan if you see him before I do. I'm sorry but I suddenly feel ill. I am going to try to get some rest. You may stay and evaluate the letter and discuss strategies to your hearts content. We'll meet again early tomorrow." He stands and looks at me once more, motioning for me to follow him.

We exit the room together and travel a short way down the wide corridor in silence. War. A feeling of guilt creeps up inside me, much like the vines in the glasshouse, taking hold and growing larger, spreading throughout me until I almost can't breath.

"I'm sorry," I say.

"Yes, so am I," he says, walking with his hands

clasped behind his back. "We have been at peace since before my father's rule. War is not a fair prospect."

"No, not that." I stop to look at him and he follows suit. "I mean, I am sorry about the war, but I'm sorry for the way I acted. I should not have caused you more distress and worry by doing and saying those things."

"Promise not to do it again and all is forgiven."

"I promise."

We begin walking once more.

"So what is it you would like to talk about?" he asks.

"Anything. Everything. What is happening in your kingdom? Cray will not be involved, I hope?"

"I do not think you came here to talk to me about the affairs of my kingdom," he answers.

"No," I admit. "It's just the only pressing thing on my mind now."

"Well, don't trouble yourself. I'm sure it will all work out. And as for Cray, I don't expect they will come to our aid."

"Why is that?"

He opens a door leading out to the garden, a back or side entrance, I'm not sure. The fragrant air catches me and takes me by surprise. It's lavender. I look around and see only hedges. Is it the lavender Stella grows that I smell?

I do not want to go back.

Prince Henry has not answered yet.

"Why do you not think Cray will come to your aid? Please answer me."

His hazel eyes that in the dark of night look almost brown stare down at me. "We are no longer allies. Your father blamed my parents for your cursing. We have not had any relations in all these years."

I am mystified by such an idea–Cray and Fallund have always been allies in my memory. I'm also relieved to hear that Cray will not be involved, but the smell of lavender alarms me. I hope desperately that Henry does not mind my company so much, because I don't plan on leaving anytime soon, no matter what potent sweetness invades my nostrils.

6
BEAST

Enough with disguises and sneaking out through the kitchen, Duncan would walk through the front castle door from now on, no matter what Henry said or who he enlisted to follow him.

Fourteen days. The girl could go to trial in fourteen days. Duncan slipped on his shoes and then took one last look in the tall mirror. Torn between whether to loathe himself for his innate distaste for royalty and hatred for its demands and responsibilities, or to be thankful for the bravery that allowed him to reject what he did not want, Duncan searched his own gaze and stature. It pained him to look in a mirror, to see so much of Henry, his own flesh and blood—his *only* flesh and blood—and know he could not back down, could never wear the robes or leadership and still keep his own soul. His greatest fear was losing himself in doing what he despised.

"Going somewhere?"

Henry's voice fractured Duncan's silent thoughts.

"No matter, Worston will follow you again. You

need at least a little protection. Do not worry for me. There are others who will fulfill your responsibilities."

Duncan turned away from the mirror; seeing both Henry and himself in the looking glass only reminded him how similar they were on the outside, nearly identical if you ignored the length of their hair, and he couldn't stare at those parallels as he declared his individuality, but facing Henry brought little improvement, since that was also like seeing his own reflection. The only difference was Henry's loss of youth. He resembled an aging man now, eyes hollow and tired, brow constantly furled. Still, he eyed his brother with determination. "I do not want to rule. I desire nothing of the kingdom, except maybe a place to sleep. If you wish, I will leave the castle and find employment."

"What on earth do you think you could do outside this castle? You have no skills, nothing to contribute..."

"I know how to work, Henry, whether you've seen it or not. And I'm good with people." He spoke calmly, falling into the place of younger brother, born only minutes after the crowned prince. Duncan thanked the stars for that. Had things been turned around, and Henry come second, they may not be having this conversation. He wondered if that would have changed him somehow, if taking on the responsibilities of ruling a kingdom would have been easier, more natural, if being born first would have made him more willing.

"Then why won't you help the people of this kingdom?"

"Why do you think that sitting on councils is the only thing I have to offer the world?"

Henry started pacing, which Duncan knew meant he was thinking, deliberating.

"Have you learned about the war?" Henry asked, still pacing with his hands clasped behind his back. His voice had faltered only slightly when saying the words and Duncan wanted to know how Henry could be so brave, how his brother could hold it together with such force and power that even with the threat of war his stone face showed no emotion, remained so unaltered.

"It was Duke who told me. I think most of the time he is the only one who can reach me. He knows where I hide when I don't want to be found, and where I go when I need to leave."

"Will you not even sit on a council when we are at war?" He stopped walking about and faced Duncan again.

"I'm not a soldier, nor a general. I know nothing of war, except to stay out of them, and I don't think that philosophy helps much when war is declared on you."

Henry took a few steps forward. Standing a few inches taller than his brother, he looked down into his eyes. "This prisoner you've taken an interest in, is she the reason you're doing all this? If you wanted to marry a peasant, Brother, why didn't you just say so?" The sarcasm cut straight through Duncan's heart. What did Henry know about her or his motives to help her or his reasons for abandoning the royal ways?

"I want to marry a peasant." Suddenly they were nine years old again, and Duncan knew if they kept at it, their communication would only get worse from here. "If you'll excuse me." Duncan headed for the door.

"You can't help her."

Henry's insistence on always getting the last word never ceased to annoy Duncan, who turned once more and simply said, "That doesn't mean I can't try."

"Just like you try so hard to be the prince you know you are."

Escaping Henry's immediate presence and the range of his voice did not mean Duncan could escape the guilt, nor the insult that his brother thought so little of him.

Winding down the tower stairs, Duncan concocted a plan. Since the prisoner was a woman, he decided a woman might be more successful at getting through to her.

He made his way to the kitchen where the maids and servants would be having breakfast. Bursting through the door, Duncan was met with a host of surprised faces, complete with open mouths and blushing cheeks. Had they been gossiping? A spread of food lay before them: fried eggs and oranges, sweet rolls and grape juice. A voice in the prince's stomach sounded, rolling like continuous, angry thunder. He ignored it.

"What is it Master Duncan?" Duke asked.

"I need to speak with Marie."

The plump woman stood obediently, her stout curls bouncing with the motion. "What is it, your majesty?" she asked.

He led her out the back kitchen entrance, the one he'd used to escape for all these years, the one that had served as his doorway to freedom.

Once outside, Duncan placed his hands on both her broad shoulders. "Marie," he began. "Thank you for taking a moment to speak with me. I'm sure this must seem so...untoward. I know that you are a mother, and that many of your children are now grown."

Marie beamed at the mention of her offspring. "Yes, your majesty."

"Well, Marie, to come right out and say it, there is a

woman, a woman I would like very much to get to know better, only this woman is different."

"Different?" Marie's scrunched up her nose and a vacant expression told Duncan he would need to be more clear.

Duncan removed his hands and turned away from Marie as he spoke. "She's...quiet, and shy. I can't get her to talk to me."

"Perhaps she does not esteem you the way you do her?"

"No, it's not that. Well, it could be. It's not that I want to get to know her in *that* way, it's that I want to help her."

"How is it you want to help her?"

Turning to face her, Duncan thought carefully about what he wanted to say. Should he reveal where she was, what she had been accused of? Should he invite Marie to come and see for herself? Perhaps that would be best. Perhaps if she saw for herself she would be more able to determine how he could help her.

"Marie, have any of your children ever been hurt? Any of your daughters?"

"Why, yes, your majesty."

"Well, I think this woman has been hurt. And I want

to do something for her. Something to cheer her up."

Marie thought a moment, looking confused. She glanced in both directions and behind her a few times before answering.

"Master Duncan, is this the woman in prison? The woman all the other servants are talking about?"

Duncan rubbed his brow. He hadn't even considered this. Here he'd been talking in code and trying to get a straight answer from her when Marie already knew.

"Yes, I am referring to the woman in prison."

Somberly, bowing her head, Marie said, "I think she needs more than cheering up, Master Duncan."

"I know she does, Marie. But it is a good place to start. Will you come with me to see her?"

"I will be serving at council meetings all day."

"Couldn't someone fill in for a couple of hours? It would mean a lot to me." He would not stoop to bribing; Marie would never take a bribe anyway.

Marie nodded and disappeared into the kitchen, returning only a few moments later with two sweet rolls, one of which she handed to the prince.

"Thank you, Marie. You are a gem." She smiled at that.

As they walked, Duncan asked her about her

children. She had seven! Four boys and three girls. The prince saw on her face the pride she had and the joy she felt in her role.

"Do you miss them?" he asked. "When you're at the castle?"

She chuckled. "Only a little. I'm always so happy to see them when I get home. And they're happy to see me."

"And your husband?" Duncan asked. "What does he do?"

"He's a leather worker." She looked at the prince's shoes. "It's possible he made those shoes you're wearing." She had a happy little walk, her stout body and shoulders shifting from side to side.

"Really? Well, if so he does marvelous work. I've had these shoes for years now." Duncan thought better than to mention he rarely wore shoes, but preferred to go barefoot, and that is most likely why his shoes lasted so long. It gladdened his heart to see her smile at the compliment.

"Here we are," Duncan said as they rounded the corner of Northeast Alley. He stopped and faced his companion. "Thank you, Marie. I am immensely grateful you came with me today."

As they walked in, the prison guard greeted them, standing promptly when he noticed the presence of royalty.

"Prince Duncan," he said.

"Hello, Thomas. Any change?" But Duncan didn't really need to ask. He could see for himself. She lay crumpled up in the same corner she'd settled into the first day.

"Oh, she got all riled up yesterday."

Duncan jerked his head to the man. "What happened?"

"We tried to give her new clothes. We brought in a woman to do it, mind you, to give her privacy. We've been taking good care of her, just like you asked. But Phillip's wife now has a black eye and claw marks down her back. He refuses to come to work now. That's why I'm here alone."

If this information frightened Marie, she did not show it. She approached the bars, but did not grasp them.

"It's all right, child. I'm not going to hurt you. I'm not even going to come inside." She turned to Duncan and began to whisper. "Is there anything you would like to know about her?"

"Her name," Duncan whispered back. "Let's start there."

"Child, do you have a name? Something we might call you by? We want to know your name." Marie had been an excellent choice. She spoke with utter gentility, her voice soft, motherly and inviting. For a moment, Duncan thought of his own mother, then suppressed the emotions following close behind.

Marie turned to the guard. "Has she spoken at all?"

"No more than incoherent screeching and angry growls."

"Do you know what happened to her?" Marie questioned further.

"All we know is that she came from Tern. Killed a Fallund man, though, or so say two witnesses."

"Two witnesses?" Duncan asked.

"Yes, your majesty. Another has come forward. Took some questioning, but he admits he saw the whole thing. Wouldn't agree to testify without the promise of a fee, but he'll do it."

"Is it still fourteen days until the court will bring her to trial?"

"Yes. Well, more like eleven now. Maybe sooner if they are able."

"Is anything else known of her?" Marie asked.

"No," Thomas answered. "But we'll keep trying, for your sake, Master Duncan."

"Thank you." Duncan wanted to go into the cell, but

knew that choice would be dangerous, not to mention risky. He didn't want to come across as a threat. "What can I do, Marie?"

"Let's go outside," Marie said, bowing her head and looking at the ground as she exited the prison and returned to the sunlit alley. She held a shawl over her forearm and faced the prince.

"Prince Duncan, I need to ask you something." Was her tone inquisitive and curious, or somber and condemning. Duncan couldn't quite tell.

"What is it, Marie?"

"Why do you want to help this woman?"

Duncan bowed his own head, searching his heart for the true answer. Why did he want to help her? He'd wondered before, but hadn't ever come up with something concrete. He would answer the best he could.

"I can't explain it completely. When I look at her, I feel something, something deep inside me, stirring and quaking. It moves me to action. You tell me, Marie. What is it I'm feeling?"

"It's compassion, Master Duncan. And it's a rare gift."

"Will you help me help her?"

"Yes. But you have to do everything I tell you to do."

"Of course I will."

"Everything." Duncan wondered why she would question him. He trusted her. Why did she feel she needed to emphasize that?

"Yes, everything," Duncan reassured.

"Okay, walk me back to the castle as I teach you the first step of getting into a heart cold as stone."

They made their way along Eastern Corridor, the corridor that would lead back to the kitchen. Duncan thought little of eating lately, but Marie's gift had been sweet and filling. "Thank you, Marie."

"Now, Master Duncan, I want you to think. Think of every possible way to get through to her. Think of all the things that a woman might like, or could like. You could try flowers, or dresses, or music. There must be something that she is fond of, even if she doesn't know it. It could be animals or carriage rides. Whatever it is, you have to find it. When you have found it, you will know, because her eyes will light up, even if only a little, and then you will know that you're on to something."

"That's it? Take her flowers?"

"It may be flowers, but it may not be. Once you find it, she will begin to open up to you. She won't be able to help it. Whatever beast has taken over, the woman is still at the heart of her. It never leaves completely."

"How do you know?"

"Because I am one."

"A beast?" Duncan asked, lifting one eyebrow high above the other.

Marie playfully whacked his arm, but it hurt more than he had expected. "You facetious prince. I meant a woman."

Duncan tilted his head back in laughter. "I know what you meant, Marie. I just couldn't help myself."

She smiled at him as they reached the castle and turned to him before going inside. "Even though you're the second born, you would make a wonderful king."

Duncan let that slap him across the face, but he would not allow it to sink into his heart. Being with Marie had lightened him, gotten his mind off the worries of the kingdom, his brother, and the woman he wanted to help.

A voice startled him from behind. "Ah, Prince Duncan, there you are."

Duncan whirled around to see Worsten, his shadow and warden, biting into a plum and subsequently dribbling juice down his face.

"Nice to see you," the prince greeted, attempting to be civil. "I hope you're up for a walk through the meadows.

I'm in need of some flowers."

"I couldn't think of a better way to spend my day." He tossed the plum pit behind him and stood at the ready, leaning forward with his hands behind his back. Duncan wanted to push him forward so he would fall on his face, but resisted the temptation.

As they hiked down Southwest Alley, Duncan offered to allow Worston the day off, promising he would never tell. All the while Worston insisted how much he enjoyed babysitting the prince. Duncan could tolerate him for now, but at the first chance of losing him, he would take it.

As they reached the meadow, Worston lay down insisting he needed a rest after the short hike from the end of Southwest Alley and across Sage Village. Hundreds of meadows could be found in Fallund, each brim with wildflowers most of the year. Even taking care to get those in full bloom, and not anything withering or dying, it didn't take long to have an armful.

Worston sat up now. "Those will die by the time we get back."

"Nonsense, you're going to go and get me a large vase filled with water and meet me back at the prison on Northeast Alley."

"Sounds like an empty hope to me."

"I command you, as your prince. Well, one of them." Duncan could barely see over all the blossoms.

"You wouldn't," Worston mumbled, a hint of a threat rolling off his tongue.

"I just did. Scurry along. I'm going to make a quick stop at a dress shop."

Worston grumbled as he stood up and began walking back down to the village, and it pleased Duncan to annoy him.

Though he'd sworn off disguises, Duncan was grateful for the flower cover when he entered one of the many dress shops along Western Corridor.

"Good day, sir," a man's voice said. "My, that is a lot of flowers. Can I have them wrapped for you?"

"That won't be necessary," Duncan answered. "I won't be long. I need you to select a dress for me, nothing too fancy, but something with color."

All too pleased, the man asked, "Well, what size would you like?"

"How am I supposed to know?"

"A-hah." The man raised a finger to the ceiling and quickened away, his feet shuffling across the floor. "I have just the thing for you. Look at these drawings." He brought back two pages. The first one showed a drawing of four women, each a different shape and height, each wearing a simple tan dress with a blue sash. "Which most looks like the shape of the girl for whom you are purchasing?"

"That one," Duncan said, nodding his head only to take in a bunch of pollen up his nose.

"This one?" the man asked, pointing to the one in the upper left corner.

"No, the one below."

"This one?"

"Yes." Not that it mattered that much. Duncan had never experienced more than a glance at her figure, which was always obscured by dim light or the position of her body.

"Very well," he said, pulling another paper in front of it. "And for her size. Would you say she is small, medium, large, or plump?"

"I don't know, medium I would guess." Prince Duncan thought of when they had lifted her into the prison cell. She was small, but strong, not tiny or scrawny at all.

"Would you like something custom made or something to go?"

"To go, please."

The man disappeared behind a counter and

returned a moment later with a straight dress the same color of purple-blue resting on some of the flowers in Duncan's hand.

"Will this do?" the man asked.

"Splendidly. Can you wrap it for me?"

"Of course, sir. And who will be paying?"

Duncan thought. He didn't usually carry coinage. "Um, charge it to the royal account."

"Your name, sir?"

"Prince Duncan." He had hoped to avoid this. Perhaps he still could. Only two other women browsed through the shop and neither had heard him. He leaned toward the man and whispered. "Let's just keep this between us. Please."

Still looking baffled, the man nodded, then stood motionless for some time.

"The wrappings, sir. Will you please wrap it for me?"

"Oh, yes, of course." Again he disappeared. Duncan glanced around him, double checking that nobody noticed him. Having never been caught outside the castle by subjects other than those he chose to reveal his identity to, he wasn't sure what their reaction would be.

His relief spilled over after leaving the dress shop.

That was not the place for him. If Henry asked again, he would tell him that he did not want to be a dressmaker. Ever.

Worston greeted him outside the prison. "Did you know your brother thinks you are mad?" he asked.

"Yes, I did," Duncan answered, forcing a polite smile. "Help me get the flowers arranged. And yes, that's an order."

Worston rolled his eyes but together they made a fine arrangement.

"Does your new dress match your eyes?" Worston asked.

Duncan ignored this comment and poked his head inside the stone archway leading down into the prison.

"Any change, Thomas?" he asked the guard.

Thomas looked up toward them from his chair, seemingly blinded by the light coming in. "None whatsoever. Sometimes I wonder if she's even breathing. But we only feed her raw meat now, and she eats some of what we give her."

Duncan looked back at Worston in time to see the sour expression on his face. Duncan would not judge her. Obviously she'd been through something hellish. Perhaps even her whole life had been torture.

Leery, Duncan walked down the stone steps and

into the dim. He approached her cell, crouched down and spoke low, hoping Worston could not hear him.

"I've brought you some flowers. And a dress. I thought perhaps you would like something other than rags to wear. But I won't mind if you don't like it."

What else was there to say? Duncan desperately hoped for some indication that she heard, that she would take them, or even just look at them. He waited for a glance, a mumble, a sigh. At this point he may even take her screaming at him. And then she moved. Only then did Duncan realize that he hadn't really been expecting her to respond. Though he wished for nothing more, he'd already accepted that she probably wouldn't. She rolled slightly onto her back, turned her head so he could see only one eye, and then pulled away again.

"That's it," he said, encouraging her to continue to acknowledge him. "I knew you could. But I won't keep you. I wish you well."

Not really wanting to go, Duncan decided it was the most likely way to gain her trust. He exited the damp of the prison to see Worston's grin.

"I wish you well?"

"Shut up, Worston," he said. "And yes, that's an order."

Duncan looked away from him and there she was, hunched over a basket across the alley, the slender, cloaked woman from before, the woman who tormented his dreams.

7
Beauty

I wake in the glass dome and sit up, alarmed by a sense that something is not right. I am alone. No flowers or vines take up the space around me. Only my bed and me exist inside the glass walls, and only the rose garden outside.

The roses!

I slide off my bed and run to the door, flinging it open. It is dark with the shade of trees, but hot, and the air is dry, sucking the moisture from my lips and mouth.

My bare feet pad across the cool, damp, packed-down dirt, stepping on a leaf or twig here and there. Everything appears fine as I run through the red roses and onto the pink. They are round and large and vibrant, holding their heads high to greet me in passing.

I reach the light purple roses next, followed by the dark. Then the orange roses, the hybrid colors, the yellow. All look alive and well, happy and full. But in the distance I can already see the drooping leaves and heads of the white roses. They sag toward the ground, their petals limp and darkening around the edges. I stop in front of them.

Why are they dying?

I look to the ground and the dirt is not damp, but dry and cracked, more like stone than fertile soil. Sorrow swells inside me, and I cannot hold back the tears. The first tear falls from my eye and lands on the dirt next to my foot, leaving a wet mark. I move to stand directly over a rose bush, and the tears come stronger now, more forcefully. They move in a steady drip, then rush out like a stream. A dark storm cloud moves over me, casting a shadow over every bit of light. It begins to rain until it pours like the sheets Stella used to whip and wave before hanging out to dry.

But a miracle happens. The roses start to lift their heads, and once they do, the clouds part to reveal a ray of sunshine, and a rainbow casts its colors above us. I smile at the flowers that had once caused me pain, happy they now look well as drops of rain slide down their petals and to their stems. While the ground appears to be mud, it still feels dry and hard beneath my feet.

A hand rests on my shoulder.

"What were you dreaming about?"

Suddenly I am not in the rose garden, but lying on a stone ground. Prince Henry stands above me, holding out a bouquet of deep purple roses.

"I know you can't take them with you, but I gathered them just the same."

He places them on the ground beside me and I sit up, wishing I could pick them up and hold them to my nose. I lean over them instead, still attempting to breath in the sweet smell of blossoming roses.

"You picked them for me? Thank you," I say, thrilled to be out of one dream and into another, one where I am with Prince Henry.

"What is it you were dreaming about?" He smiles mysteriously, as if holding onto a secret.

"Why?" I ask, suddenly self conscious. Had I been drooling? Father always used to tell me I drooled in my sleep. And talked. Oh, please tell me I wasn't talking.

"You were smiling." He sits down on the bench beside me.

"I was?" Relieved, I try to remember where I'd been before. Ah yes, the roses. "Oh, I was in a rose garden, the one outside the hot house where I'm fast asleep." It feels strange to be talking about where my body is, when my mind is clearly someplace else.

"Your parents put you in a hot house?" He leans back on one hand and takes a bite of a plum with the other.

"Why would they do that?"

I bow my head, feeling ashamed of the truth, whatever the truth may be, for I've only ever speculated as to why they've done this. "I like to think it was because it was too painful to have me so close to them, so accessible." I look up to Henry, wanting to take a bite of the real food he holds so carelessly in his hand, so taken for granted. "I imagine them coming to see me in my bedroom often those first few months, caught up in their sorrow and grieving, until finally they knew it was time to move on."

"I'm sorry." He takes one more large bite of the plum and then tosses the remains into a nearby shrub. "Does it pain you to talk about them?"

"Yes," I admit openly. "I hate to think of them mourning me when I am not dead to be mourned. Does that make any sense?"

He leans forward now, placing both hands on the edge of the bench. "Perhaps you should be grateful that your parents are still alive."

The words sting me, cutting me through the center. "How can you say something so cruel to me?"

"My parents are dead." He speaks it without any emotion. A simple accepted fact.

I search my memory for some knowledge of this.

The king and queen of Fallund? Dead? No, this is news to me. "I'm sorry," I say, for nothing else comes to mind.

An uncertain silence stands between us. Had he slept the night outside in the garden? The thought of asking him this question mortifies me. Thankfully, he begins to explain.

"You've been out here for some time now. It's been two days since our last conversation. My guess is that you're not leaving anytime soon. Whenever I come down in the morning, here you are, sleeping."

I process this slowly, wondering at the possibility of such a notion, that a part of me is choosing to stay in this garden so I am close to him, and then another part of me wanders off in the strange dreams of my deeper sleep.

"Oh," I say, feeling stupid, and revealed in some personal way. Too personal.

"And thanks to you, half my council thinks I'm crazy."

"They do?"

"Oh, yes. All sorts of rumors are scurrying about the castle like mice, including rumors about my—" He leans in close to me with a hand guarding his mouth as if to keep anybody else from seeing or hearing what he's about to say, and then whispers, "Garden conversations with imaginary beings."

He's being playful, and I'm grateful he doesn't seem to be angry with me. "Ah," I say. "Well you may tell them that I don't think you're crazy."

He scoffs at the idea. "I don't think I'll be telling anyone about you. I'm not even sure I believe you're really here."

This hurts even more than his comment about my parents. Can't he see me? And hear me? Isn't that proof enough?

"I know what will cheer you up," he says. "In a short while I'll be meeting with my council." He is teasing me, smiling undoubtedly about my behavior in the last meetings.

Briefly I remember our discussion about war, and how my kingdom blames him for my curse and withholds support for revenge. "I don't think I want to go to your council meeting."

"I'll let you play with Covington's moustache," he entices. He must see that I don't want to come, and I think he must really want me there because now he looks solemn. "I'll be in this meeting for most of the day. I'd be honored if you joined me. I may not be at liberty to acknowledge your presence, but I will listen to any thoughts you may have." He avoids my eyes now, and stares down to the roses still resting on the ground. "And I would love to have your company."

Suddenly I'm five years old again, and feel as though Father has invited me on one of his sea voyages. I can't help smiling now, despite the prospect of war. "I'd be honored as well. Thank you for the invitation."

He picks up the bouquet of roses and leads me inside, where he hands the flowers off to Marie, instructing her to put them in a vase and bring them up to the council chamber. He ignores her questioning stare.

We climb the tower stairs and I marvel at how the main level below gets smaller and smaller as we climb. I follow him, eased by his confidence as we reach the chamber to find men are already arriving. Duke waits outside the door and Henry asks him if Duncan will be attending. Duke shakes his head in answer.

"Who's Duncan?" I ask.

He leans close to me and makes sure nobody is watching him. Even Duke is distracted by the maids arranging the cart outside. "He's my brother."

A vague memory comes to mind, voices outside the castle the night I'd come by carriage. Prince Duncan. I let the name roll off my tongue a time or two. It feels familiar, safe. I like him already even though we've never met.

"Gentlemen, if you'll be seated, I'd like to get started immediately." Henry takes his place at the center of the far, long side of the table, directly across from the sea painting. Marie enters with a cart full of food, tea, and the vase of deep purple roses which she places at one end of the table.

A few of the men whisper. One comments on how lovely the flowers look, clearly amused by the idea of flowers in a council meeting. Henry ignores them.

"I trust you've all had the opportunity to read the letter and brainstorm possible solutions. I would like to hear any ideas you have. We'll start to my right."

The stout man who always sits next to Henry gives his opinion. "We must ask for support form Cray."

I am standing in front of the painting. Henry looks at me and we exchange a glance before he turns back to his council member.

"What do you mean?"

"I am under the impression that without help from Cray, we do not stand a chance in a war against Tern. Their armies are too large. And it may be a trick. Perhaps they have actually enlisted the help of the barbarians to fight against us. They may seek help from Cray eventually anyway. It would be better for us to restore them as allies before Tern gets to them."

Henry leans back in his chair and rubs his chin. Can he see the terror on my face? I do not want Cray fighting in any war.

"They can give us the advantage in many ways," another voice adds. A man I'd never seen before, his dark eyes and tight jacket catch my attention, as does his unusually long hair. "They can give us sea cover, and if they allow us to cut through their lands, we will not have to go through the barbarians to get to Tern."

"Form an alliance," Henry says, musing. "Or, restore one, that is." He looks at me again.

I shake my head at him. As much as I would love the alliance to be restored, I do not want Father fighting in any war, and I know he will not allow his people to fight unless he is at the lead.

He looks around the room, seemingly at each individual face of his council men, and then always back to me. Is he hoping I'll express my opinion?

"Well, I vote no!"

A smile forms on his lips.

"Do you find this amusing, Prince Henry?" one of the men asks.

Henry clears his throat and sits up taller in his chair, scooting it closer to the table as well. "No. Just puzzling. I am thinking on it. I hadn't considered asking Cray for help, assuming of course that they are still at odds with us because of the sleeping curse placed on Princess Eglantine."

A few of the men begin to laugh. "Does Prince Henry still believe in fairy stories?" one of them asks, still chuckling.

I glare at him.

Henry looks at me for a reaction. Is he concerned for my feelings? Well, if he is, he will keep Cray out of his war.

"Are there any other ideas?" Henry asks.

Growing more frightened with each moment of silence following, I start to breathe heavily, terrified of the prospect. I think of Father and almost as soon as I do I think I hear his voice. Could it be time for them to visit me again? It doesn't seem like enough time has passed.

I am not ready to go back. "Say something," I say to Henry.

"What would you like me to say?"

It takes a moment before he realizes he's said it out loud and now all the council men look at him expectantly.

"Say you'll ask for support from the king of Cray," one of them answers.

No, anything but that. "Say something," I repeat.

"There must be another solution."

Henry tries to pretend he can't hear me and clears his throat before investigating further. "What does our army look like?"

Everyone looks to the end of the table closest to the door, the one opposite my roses. "Commander?" Henry asks. "What does our army look like?"

The commander leans forward, thoughtful. "Well, they train regularly, practice fighting techniques, and learn war strategies, but they've never had real experience."

A quiet murmur spreads throughout the room. "And they're young. Average age is twenty-one."

"You see, Prince Henry," the stout man on Henry's right says. "It is foolish to go into this war alone. We have no other allies."

"Is it really that hopeless? Is that really all you have?" Henry asks, throwing his arms up in the air. I am equally disappointed at their lack of creativity. "I'll be writing a correspondence to the king of Tern later today. Please tell me we can come up with at least one more alternative plan."

Some of the men exchange glances.

"No?" Henry questions once more. "Fine. Then you will sit here until you come up with something else."

A common groan sounds now.

"We'll take a recess for a few minutes. Please help yourselves to some nourishment. You're going to need it."

I hear Mother's voice now. She is laughing. Curious, I try to listen in without losing my hold on the sight of Henry, nor the sound of his voice.

"If you'll excuse me," Henry says, standing up and walking toward the door.

Stella laughs now. "I knew it would happen." Her voice is faint, so distant I wonder if I'm slipping into another layer of dreaming rather than hearing her for real.

I feel a kiss on my cheek, and the wet warmth of hot tears. Startled that I will lose Henry if I do not stay with him, I follow him out the door.

He paces back and forth, running his hands through his hair until it is quite messy.

"You need a comb now," I tell him.

"What?" He looks at me.

"Your hair." I nod toward the stacked mess on his head.

"Oh, right." He settles it back down with his fingers. "What am I going to do?" He had asked the ground, as if the ground would tell him, but I take it as a sign that he wants to know what I think.

"I think you'll do the right thing."

"Eglantine," Father says. "Eglantine, can you hear me?"

I turn away from Henry for a moment, looking up to my right. I want to tell him that yes, I do hear him, but that I can't listen to him right now. "It's your mother," he says.

Henry says something but it isn't until he's finished that I realize I hadn't been listening. "I'm sorry, what did you say?" I ask.

"Eglantine, your mother is going to have a baby." He starts to cry. I've never seen Father cry, but I can hear him now, practically sobbing.

Henry repeats himself, but again I do not hear it. I lean my ear toward Father, or at least, toward where I believe him to be, sitting by my right side. Instinctively, I lie down.

"Eglantine, what are you doing?" Henry asks.

"Something's happened. My mother's expecting a baby."

"Eglantine, you're not leaving, are you? Please stay here," Henry says.

"The spell, Eglantine. The spell will be broken," Father continues. He grabs my hand and leans forward to kiss me, his cheeks gruff and scratchy. I jerk as several of his tears fall onto my face.

"Eglantine, please don't go." Henry sounds urgent now. I am torn between whether to celebrate with my family, or stay with the one person that will give me any interaction.

"Darling, it's true." Aunt Cornelia isn't crying. She sounds ecstatic, overjoyed. "You'll be awake again. And we'll do all the things we've missed out on all these years."

"Shhhh," Stella whispers. "You're disturbing her. She's beginning to shake. Stand back, I'm going to administer some tonic."

"No!" I say.

"No, you won't stay?" Henry asks.

Henry, I'd forgotten all about Henry. But I know he can't help me. It's too late. Stella will give me the tonic and I'll be dreaming that I'm in a dream...in a dream...in a dream.

"Eglantine, wait." It is the last I hear of Henry's voice.

"Redelia, hold her other hand," Stella says. The liquid runs down my throat and nearly gags me. I cough and sputter, turning onto my side. Mother lets go of my hand as I pull it away so I can lie on my stomach.

"Oh, I hate to see her like this," Mother says, and I imagine her putting her hands over her eyes. "I can't stand it." She begins to cry. I wonder if she realizes how much those words hurt me, how much I wish she would bear it with a little more courage, a little more acceptance.

Suddenly it's black as night, and I'm standing in a thick forest filled with panic, terrified that I will see her shortly—the witch who cursed me—and she will chase me through the woods until I realize the woods have no end.

8
BEAST

Duncan stared through the prison bars at the girl in the corner. If nothing else, at least she was eating, even if it was a strip of raw fish. Duncan hadn't yet discovered what it was that she loved, what would open her up a bit. She'd ripped the dress to shreds and pulled every single flower off its stem, not to mention shattered the vase then licked the water off the ground.

He watched her as she knelt there, holding the fish to her mouth and violently tearing the meat apart with her teeth. She seemed to enjoy it as much as the deer and pheasant she'd been given previously.

Today, Duncan had brought some paper, quills and an inkwell. He reached his hands through the bars, holding onto the gifts he offered her. She looked up from her meal, jerking back at his forward motions.

"It's all right," Duncan said. "I'm not going to hurt you. Do you like to draw? Or maybe write some poetry?"

He thought it sounded so foolish coming out of his mouth. How could such a creature love such things? Had she ever even seen anything like them before?

"I'm just going to set them down here, and then you can use them if you'd like."

She continued to twitch, dropping the fish and backing away.

"Please don't be frightened. I only want to help you."

The girl began breathing heavily, huffing and growling. Duncan released the treasures and pulled his hands out of the bars. She rolled back onto her feet, crouched low and swaying back and forth.

Duncan knew he'd done it now. Something had set her off. He quickly reached his arm in again to retrieve the offensive items and she came after him, staying low to the ground and yelling incoherently. Duncan pulled his arm out just in time to prevent the tragedy of having it torn off by the wild beast. She reached the bars and let out a loud, animalistic roar, following which she tore up all the paper and threw the inkwell, hitting Duncan directly on the chest. Ink spilled out and ran down his shirt and breeches. He thought it ironic that now he actually wore normal clothing when going outside the castle, it should get destroyed.

He turned toward the guard and said, "That went well."

Met with nothing but laughter, Duncan walked

toward the exit. "I think I'll go and get cleaned up a bit." Glancing back at her, the prince saw her inspecting the quills, as if she knew not to destroy a feather, but could not figure out what the use of this particular feather was.

The guard stopped laughing momentarily. "Perhaps you should bring someone to sing to her, a minstrel. Or a jester. Everyone loves to laugh."

"I highly doubt its entertainment that she wants."

"What then?" the prison guard asked.

"I don't know." Duncan walked away, and determined not to be discouraged, he thought of more ideas. Perhaps she did like to be sung to, or to listen to an instrument being played. Duncan had yet to try animals as well. She was wild after all. A dog or a bunny might be just the thing to begin earning her trust. Or she might snap its neck and sink her teeth into it.

On his way back to the castle, Duncan thought of nothing else. He knew there had to be a way. Could Marie have been wrong, and all these attempts at finding something the woman was interested in merely a waste of precious time?

Once in his bedroom, Duncan changed his clothing, selecting a similar outfit to the ink-stained one. He buttoned it while standing in front of a mirror hanging on his wall.

Then he noticed something sitting on the writing desk behind him, a reflection of something he knew hadn't been there before. Turning around, Duncan walked toward the desk by the window, still buttoning the front of his shirt. A brush lay atop the desk. The prince couldn't remember ever using a brush. His hair wasn't long enough to need one. Had Marie brought it?

Something else rested atop the desk, an envelope with his name on it. Curious, he opened it, finding a letter addressed to him on top of another piece of parchment.

"Master Duncan," it began.

Duncan glanced to the closing of the letter to see who had penned it. Karl's signature was found at the bottom of the page. The short message simply asked him to read the enclosed.

Duncan read the letter, addressed to the king of Fallund, and as he did, an unquenchable anger filled him. How could his brother have been so stupid? What was all this talk of war? He set the letter down and took long strides to his wardrobe, selecting a clean pair of shoes. After going back for the letter, and also picking up the silver handled hairbrush, Duncan stormed out of his room and straight to the council chamber room below.

"Have you seen this?" Duncan asked his brother

after bursting through the door.

Henry squinted at him. "What is it?"

"Well, it's not a declaration of war, I can tell you that much."

"What on earth are you talking about?" Henry began reading again which only fueled Duncan's anger.

"I want you to stop that. Stop reading and listen to me."

Henry slammed his book shut. "Very well, Brother. What is it?"

"This is not a declaration of war." Duncan waved the letter in front of him.

Henry stood and walked toward his brother, looking annoyed, perhaps even guilty. Grabbing the letter out of Duncan's hands, he only needed to glance at it before he knew what it was.

"Well if it isn't a declaration of war, then what is it? I am glad you finally decided to share your opinion on this." Henry spat the words, his own anger coming out and it filled Duncan with remorse. Only if he'd gone to one of those council meetings, he may have prevented all of this.

"It is an invitation for peace and alliance."

"How can you be so naive?" Henry yelled. "It clearly threatens war. It's an open invitation."

"No, look." Duncan grabbed the parchment back from him and pointed to the words as he read. "We have no choice but to bring slaughter onto the barbarians. They are spreading innumerably, entering our lands and causing chaos wherever they reach. If you refuse to assist us in this effort, we will not be responsible for any of your countrymen that find themselves in our way."

"I fail to see the invitation for peace."

"Henry you must write to him. Write to him and tell him we will help him fight the barbarians. It will be easily done. They have few weapons, and even those are mostly used for hunting their food. They are uneducated. We will not lose many lives." Duncan pleaded with his brother, hoping to find some success before it was too late.

"Look who's suddenly the expert on Tern, foreign relations, war and barbarians." Henry spoke calmly, his arms folded across his chest.

"I attended lessons same as you. Remember?"

"Of course I remember. I just thought you didn't care." The words were intended to sting. Duncan could see it in his brother's eyes. He had wanted to hurt him with his words.

"Well you were wrong. I do care. And I am opposed to this war. Unequivocally. It is folly."

"It's too late," Henry said. "I already sent correspondence. We are preparing for war. We have to at least defend ourselves. If they make war on the barbarians, then our lands will be overrun."

"Well at least write to Cray for help then."

Just then the door opened and Duke walked in, eyeing both the princes with a look of suspicion. "Is everything all right Master Henry?"

Duncan ran his hand through his hair as he watched his brother perform the same act simultaneously.

"Yes, Duke. Everything is fine," Henry said.

"Why are you doing this?" Duncan asked.

After deducing that Henry was not going to answer him, Duncan turned to leave. He crumpled the letter and threw it over the balcony. Filled with rage, he wanted to throw the hairbrush as well, but restrained himself. How could his brother be so stupid?

Henry and Duke continued the conversation without him and Duncan listened to their words.

"I'm angry that he refuses to attend council meetings, and then has the audacity to come in here and tell me I'm in the wrong. Where was he the night we met to discuss this?" Poor Duke. Now he was getting scolded for Duncan's behavior.

Duncan moved closer to the door, placing his ear near the crack to hear better. "Calm down, Master Henry. I'm sure he means well."

"Why can't he realize that I don't need another council member or aide? All I really need is a brother by my side. Doesn't he have any idea how lonely and taxing this job is without him?"

Duncan peeked through the crack to see Henry sit down at the table. Duke stood beside him. "I imagine not, your highness."

Pulling back, Duncan walked away, steadily picking up his pace until he was running down the tower stairs and out to the garden where the first thing he saw was Worston's face. He couldn't contain it any longer. He felt as thought he would explode.

"Hello, Master Duncan. Just the prince I was looking for. You're a hard fellow to find these days. Oh, what a lovely hairbrush–"

Without warning, and further angered by Worstn's teasing, Duncan threw his fist into the man's face. Worston fell backward at the blow, covered his eye and nose, and then scrambled to his feet.

"What was that for?" he asked.

"Wrong place, wrong time," Duncan answered. "And

don't follow me today. That's an order."

Worston backed away to let the prince past, placing his free hand up in a gesture of surrender. Duncan glanced back at him, feeling only a little sorry for what he'd done.

Walking quickly, he allowed Henry's words to sink in. He hadn't wanted another council member or aide? Just a brother?

The prince had to force himself to breathe, in and out, in and out, until he felt calm enough to turn the quick breaths into slower and slower ones. As the anger seeped away some, Duncan allowed the guilt to flood in. This was all his fault. All his refusing to attend meetings and dodging his brother and escaping the castle. It had all added up to a war that didn't really need to happen. And it was all his fault.

Duncan thought of the army, probably on full alert now, training daily. How many of them would die needlessly because of his selfishness, his refusal to step up and be who he'd been born to be. But what about Henry? Even he had refused the title of King, even though he was the rightful heir. All the kingdom still referred to him as Prince Henry. After the king and queen had died, still in mourning and overwhelmed with his new responsibilities, Henry had postponed any coronation, making one excuse after another for over five years now. Was he hoping

Duncan would step up and be king, the second born, if only by minutes?

Feeling sluggish now, and overwhelmed by a sense that he'd failed not only his brother and family, but the entire kingdom, Duncan twirled the brush in his hands. Had all of this obsession over the prison girl caused this? Should he stop going to see her?

Looking down, Duncan did not notice someone stood in front of him until he saw two bare feet, covered in part by a long, wide dress of palest yellow, patterned with tiny flowers and draped with a black cloak.

Suddenly frightened, Duncan looked at her face, the woman from his dreams. Despite his fear, Duncan confronted her. "Who are you?" he asked.

"It does not matter who I am," she said.

"Are you following me?"

"Yes," she answered. Wishing he hadn't asked that question (because she'd given the answer he hadn't wanted to hear) Duncan thought of how much better it would be to have Worston tracking him.

"May I see it?" she asked, holding out her hand.

Not wanting to, but afraid of what she might do if he didn't, Duncan held out the brush for her. She took it and caressed it, held it up to her face, ran it through her own hair and afterwards cleaned out the bristles with her long, bony fingers. Finally, she turned it around and kissed the back of it.

After handing it back to Duncan, she walked away, the rear of her cloak trailing behind her in the dirt.

Rounding the corner of Northeast Alley, Duncan walked straight to the prison, baffled by what he'd just experienced. He stepped down to the prison and greeted the guard who'd been there earlier. "Hello, Ben."

"Good day, Prince Duncan. What have you brought with you this time?"

Duncan smiled at him, then put a finger to his lips, a silent invitation for the man to be quiet. "Will you give me some time alone with her? Please?" he whispered.

Looking confused, and uncertain whether he should give in or not, the man asked "Where shall I go?"

"Just wait outside."

The guard nodded and Duncan thanked him.

"Hello," Duncan called quietly as he approached the bars. "I brought you something." He took slow steps, being cautious not to make too much noise. "I thought you might like to brush your hair. And you may keep it if you'd like."

She looked up at him from the floor, and as she did the sun coming through the window shone on her face.

Scratch marks covered her cheeks as well as her arms. What on earth had she done to herself?

As she caught a glimpse of the hairbrush, Duncan saw something in her eyes. A memory? A light? He couldn't quite tell what it meant, but it was something.

"Would you like to hold it?" he asked.

Never making eye contact, she stood up. Duncan waited for her to get closer, not wanting to put his hands through the bars unless she seemed calm and not likely to take a bite out of him.

Her dirt and blood-stained hands gripped the bars, her eyes all the while focusing on the object in Duncan's hands. He held it out for her, still staying almost an arm's reach away from her cell.

Twitching, she looked away, as if checking to see whether they were alone or if someone was sneaking up behind her. Then without warning, she snatched it from the prince's hand, clanging it loudly against the bars. But she did not retreat. Seemingly enthralled, she caressed it much as the old woman had done outside. After a moment, she held it back out to Duncan. He took it from her, pleased with the interaction and not wanting to hurt her feelings or do or say the wrong thing. "Do you like it?"

She stood there, still focusing on the brush, but now

she held onto a piece of hair, smoothing it over in one hand followed by the other. Over and over she ran the hair through her fingers.

Henry held the brush back out to her again. "Would you like to try it?"

She took it from him and then handed it right back, pointing it toward Duncan's chest.

"What is it?" Duncan asked. "Do you want *me* to do it?" His heart skipped a nervous beat at the thought, and his mouth suddenly became dry.

No answer escaped her lips, just the same playing with a piece of her hair.

Duncan considered what to do. On the one hand, if she actually wanted him to come in there and brush her hair, he had done it: found the thing that would win her over. On the other, if he went in there, he might not come out in one piece.

"Just give me a minute," he said, holding it out to her once more. "Here, you hold this and I'll go and get the key."

It took some persuasion, not to mention a lecture about the risks, but Ben handed over the key.

When Duncan reached her again, she was inspecting the silver handle. Upon seeing him, she held it out once more. "Oh, thank you," he said, taking it back from her. "Just let me get a chair." He pulled the guard's chair across the floor and as he did so, she looked startled and began to twitch again. Duncan stopped. "It's all right. I'm going to open the door and bring the chair inside with me. Then, if you'd like, you may sit on the chair and I will brush your hair."

She calmed somewhat, but still looked leery.

"Will you please stand back from the door?" He asked it just in case she meant to escape, and to his surprise, she listened.

With her standing at a distance, Duncan unlocked the door and went inside. After placing the chair inside the bars, he closed the door, reached his hands back out and locked himself inside with her, hoping it wouldn't be his last action. Ben watched from the door as Duncan tossed the keys out of reach.

"Now," he said, placing the chair in the sunlight. "Would you like to sit down?"

Still holding onto a piece of hair, she approached slowly, all the while keeping her eyes either on the hairbrush, or Ben who still watched from outside. She turned just in time to lower herself onto the seat. Amazed, and filled with a giddy excitement, Duncan closed his eyes, breathing a sigh of relief.

Starting at the bottom, Duncan began working his way up through the snarls. Her hair felt greasy, and crusted, but it worked like magic, smoothing it out almost instantly, with no indication that it caused her any pain.

The prince lost himself in the act of providing this service for her, feeling her long hair between the fingers of his free hand, holding a chunk of hair gently and smoothing the part that hung free, protecting her scalp from the pulling and tugging. Had this been the same girl he'd seen earlier? Roaring and ripping up parchment, not to mention chucking an inkwell at his chest.

It took the better part of an hour, but her hair now hung to the middle of her back, long, loose and free. Duncan did not stop, but continued to brush as long as she let him.

"I didn't murder anyone," she said.

The words cut through the silence, shocking the prince into stillness. Still holding a section of hair in one hand, he racked his brain, not knowing what to say.

Before responding, Duncan began brushing again, hoping the continuous motion would keep her calm. "Then why do some say you did?"

"Well, I did kill a man. But it wasn't murder. He got what was coming to him."

What did that mean? She'd killed out of self defense? Had it been part of her way of life with the barbarians? How could he make her understand that either way, it really didn't matter.

Duncan paused again, formulating his words carefully. He spoke softly and slowly, hoping to convey that he was on her side. "Whether you murdered someone or not, most will think your punishment is just."

Waiting for a reaction, Duncan watched her hands in her lap, totally calm, the blood on her arms dry and crusted. "So be it then," she said.

A weight of discouragement fell over him, the discouragement he'd been resisting since morning. It seemed he could do nothing right. Was it all hopeless? The girl? The kingdom? Restoring any sort of relationship with his brother?

"Thank you for letting me brush your hair," he said. Calling to Ben, Duncan prepared to leave, placing the treasure in the girl's lap.

Ben opened the cell and Duncan exited, a relief falling over him once the door had been locked again. There she sat, staring at the gift. A cloud outside rolled over the sun and the light that had once been shining on her vanished. "What happened to her face and arms?" Duncan asked.

"It was the quill, sire. She experimented with it on her skin for a time, then finally threw it through the bars. I'm sorry. I didn't dare go in and stop her."

Duncan placed a hand on his shoulder. "I understand Ben. Send word if there are any changes."

"Sire, the chair," Ben said in a bit of a whine.

He hadn't really done it on purpose, but was now glad that he'd locked it in with her. She deserved a place to sit. "Well if you want it, go in and get it." Prince Duncan smiled at his own joke, though it was clear Ben hadn't found it amusing. "I'll send another. Leave it be."

Braving one last glance, Duncan found that she no longer focused her attention on the hairbrush, but looked directly at him. He smiled at her, not sure if it was the proper reaction, but it felt like the natural thing to do. Did she smile back at him? He couldn't be sure.

Walking up the steps and onto the dusty road, Duncan looked up only to be pelted on the face with fierce drops of rain. Undeterred, he stepped out, beginning a brisk walk back to the castle, feeling all the while as though someone followed.

9

Beauty

The memory of the forest lingers in my mind. Incapable of escape, and terrified that she will find me, I keep my eyes shut, and pretend I am a caterpillar in a cocoon.

It is dark, but I am safe.

I imagine myself wrapped up, hanging from a leaf that is both obliging and kind. I pretend I am invisible to her. I refuse to open my eyes.

"Eglantine!"

It is a desperate cry, but distant, like listening to the ocean from inside the castle. It is Henry.

I do not dare open my eyes, fearful it is a trick, the witch in disguise, the focal point of all my dark dreams.

"Eglantine, where are you?"

I hug my legs to my chest, squeezing my eyes shut even tighter, wrapping my arms tight around my ankles. I am a caterpillar. I am a caterpillar. I am a caterpillar.

His voice is closer now. "Eglantine, I need to speak

with you. Please come back."

I can hear the frustration, the tendency to give up easily, and I imagine him running his hand through his hair, turning from me and walking away. I do not want him to leave.

"Don't go," I yell, still refusing to look.

"Eglantine, are you there?" I imagine him turning toward my voice. Where is he? In the castle? In our meeting spot in the garden? I cannot look. I tuck my head into my chest. She could be there waiting for me if I open my eyes.

"Eglantine, I want to ask you something."

What could Henry have to ask me? I imagine all this eager calling my name is because he simply wants more advice. Should he go to war? It is not worth opening my eyes. He will have to figure it out on his own.

"Eglantine, listen to me." It sounds as though he is sitting down, perhaps on the bench near the row of hedges, or even on the ground, the grass rustling beneath him. Yes, I think he is on the ground. He doesn't want anyone to see him talking to me because I am nothing.

"Eglantine." He's whispering now. He is ashamed of me, and I want to crawl out of my cocoon and into a hole, to be buried alive. What difference would it make now after all these years? I am as good as dead anyway. And the prospect of a baby does not comfort me as it did my parents. Perhaps they cannot admit it, but it might not even be a boy. I will not so foolishly get my hopes up as they have.

"Eglantine, is everything all right? I haven't seen you for days. So much has happened. I have something I want to ask you, but I want it to be in person."

In person? Not possible.

"I mean, as in person as two people can be when one of them is dreaming." He sighs. "Sometimes I think I was dreaming too. And I fear you will never come back."

His words touch me, deep in my soul. He is afraid of me not coming back, and I hear the sorrow in his voice at the prospect. Could my presence mean that much to him? And if so, why?

"I thought I heard your voice. Are you here somewhere? Please answer if you are."

"I want to be here," I say.

"There, I heard you again. Where are you?" He's standing now. I hear him move in the grass. But if I can hear him in the grass, does that mean I am in the garden with him? It could still be a trick. His voice is above me now. "Where are you?"

"I'm in a forest."

"Which forest? I will come to you."

I ache at the thought of what my answer must be. "Henry, it is not a real forest."

"Oh, what's it like then?" I imagine him sitting again, on the bench this time.

"It's dark."

"Is it night time in your dream? It's well after daybreak here."

"I don't know."

"Well, is the sun up? Or the moon? Are there stars?"

"I don't know. My eyes are closed. I'm afraid to open them."

"Afraid? What could you have to be afraid of? You're dreaming."

He's making fun of me, but I know it's because he doesn't understand. "Just because I'm dreaming, doesn't mean it's not real for me. It's all I know."

"Open your eyes," he whispers.

The prospect of seeing Henry tempts me to open my eyes. But should I do it? Will I regret it?

"Please, Eglantine. Open your eyes."

I draw my head away from my chest. It does seem lighter, like the night and dark of the forest are gone. I begin with the tiniest little crack, lifting my left eyelid just enough to see a blur of my immediate surroundings. I see my white nightgown, bright in the morning sun, and a hedge, blocking my view of anything else. I open both eyes now.

The forest is gone.

The night is over.

I roll onto my back and turn to my other side, and there he is, sitting on the bench as I had first predicted, leaning forward so his elbows rest on his legs, and clasping his hands.

"Isn't that better?" he asks.

I sit up and face him. It is good to see him, but I do not smile. It would be forced today. I do not feel joyful, or happy. I feel alone, and imprisoned in a world that is not genuine, and therefore not worthwhile.

"It's good to see you," he says. "But you look unhappy."

I do not cry often in my sleep, but it has happened before: when I dream of Father or Mother dying; or sometimes the smell of the lilies brings a mist to my eyes; or when I dreamt of the rose garden and watering it with my tears. I know the tears are authentic when I actually feel them on my face. A tear wets my cheek now.

"Eglantine, what's wrong?" He inspects me further,

leaning toward where I sit on the grass. "Are you crying?"

I wipe the tear.

He slips off the bench and kneels in front of me. "Eglantine," he whispers. "I don't know why you're crying. I understand if you don't want to talk about it, but I have something I'd like to ask you. Will you listen to me?"

I nod, grateful that he will not force me to answer him, wanting to hear what he has to say rather than focus on my own pitiful state.

"Eglantine, we are going to war. We leave this night for encampment."

I immediately think of Father.

"Do not worry. Cray has not become involved."

"Well, what is it you want to ask me?"

He bows his head, a heavy sigh escaping his mouth.

"What is it?" I ask. "Why do you hesitate?"

Looking up at me again, and reaching out for my hand as if he could actually grab a hold of it, he answers. "I hesitate because I do not want you to think I am weak. And I would never ask this of you under normal circumstances. But since you are sleeping . . . safely . . . and only here because of some phenomenon that neither of us can explain. Since you can't be hurt while you're here, and nobody else can see you . . ."

I watch his hand, reaching out to me, and try to grasp it with my own. I know it is not possible, but I make the motion anyway. "What?" I ask. "What is it you would like me to do?" In all of my imagination I cannot think of what he is trying so desperately to ask me.

"Will you come? Please? Come with me and keep me company as I go to war?"

Baby beads of sweat begin to take shape on his forehead. How vulnerable he has made himself; I can see it in his eyes, their longing and anticipation. He is shaking now, both his hands cupped around mine.

"Please."

I imagine traveling with him. How will I learn to stay at his side? What if I wake in the castle or the garden and he is nowhere to be found? Then I think of the far worse horrors that may be. What if I am forced to watch him die?

A nervousness crawls up my stomach and clenches my throat. I try to swallow, and notice for the first time how dry my mouth is.

"I would never ask if–"

"I know," I say, cutting him off, not able to listen to his pleas any longer. "I know you wouldn't."

"So will you come?"

"Yes," I say. I barely hear it, but I feel it go through

my lips and teeth, forced out by my parched tongue. And I mean it. I will go with him. I want to.

"Yes?" he asks, as if he hadn't quite heard it either and needs the reassurance.

"Yes," I say, louder, more firmly. "I will come. I will stay by your side as long as I am welcome and able to do so."

"If you get lost I will come looking for you, as I did this morning. I will call your name until you come."

"They'll think you're crazy." I am closer to smiling than I have been since I left him last.

"They already do." He smiles easily, and I think of how grand a smile it is, especially considering the circumstances that lie before him. War. I know little of it, except what I heard Father talk of as a child, what I've seen in my dreams, or what Stella has read to me. There is, however, something in particular I remember. In most of my dreams, colors are dampened, as if everything is laid over with a thin cloth of brown, black or gray. But I've dreamt of wars where everything was black and white. Everything, except the blood, which ran in pools of both deep and bright red. It seemed hot, a steam lifting from it that never cooled, never stopped rising.

In all my years of sleeping I have not felt what I do

now: needed. A sense of pleasure fills me up, and I begin to shiver, feeling cold with excitement.

He stares at me still, looking at my eyes, which must be faint, nearly invisible, but he doesn't seem to notice. "Thank you," he says. "Stay close." Releasing his pretend hold on my hands, he pushes up from the grass and leads me toward the castle.

Walking through the castle doors is a different experience today. We are met with a buzz that I've never heard before, and Henry is immediately bombarded.

"Did you have a nice reprieve in the garden, Master Henry?" Duke asks.

"Yes, thank you."

"Your highness, we're ready to discuss the final strategy now. All the men are waiting in the council chamber." It is the stout man, the one who always sits to Henry's right.

"Thank you, Bern."

Bern looks as though he hasn't slept in a week, the circles under his eyes darker than night.

"Is Duncan there?"

"No, your majesty."

"Master Duncan went out this morning. Worston brought me word. He's at the prison, but should return again soon. Perhaps he'll come then."

Henry nodded. "Perhaps. Thank you, Duke."

"After you, your majesty." Bern gestures to the hallway before him, signaling it is time for the prince to move forward. I sense his hesitation, and think of the weight he must be carrying now. He looks to me and I smile in encouragement before he leads the way down the halls filled with people running about. I look back to see Bern stopping for a moment. He whispers with a man about outfitting the prince and how the weaponry is being delivered to the castle.

We climb the tower stairs. Well, they climb, I seem to be floating. We stop outside the council chamber doors where Marie and two other maids are putting the finishing touches on a serving cart.

"Gentlemen, Marie, if you please, I would like another moment before going in."

Bern lets out a loud, annoyed huff as he walks through the door.

"Of course, your majesty," Duke says as he uses his hands to direct Marie and the cart inside. The other maids scurry off quickly down the tower stairs.

Henry is taking quick breaths. He runs a hand through his hair as he turns away from me.

"No turning back now," I say. "It's time to go in there."

He faces me. "Do you think I've made a big mistake?"

"What do you mean?"

"Never mind," he says, shaking his head. "You're right. It's time to go in." Before he pushes the door open, he pauses, facing me once more. "Eglantine, thank you again. I can't tell you how much it means to have you here."

I nod, first at him, and then toward the door, encouraging him to go through it.

At first, I barely recognize it. The table has been pushed up against the far wall and is covered with stacks of parchment. Behind it, a map of the region is pinned to the wall. Chairs which once circled the table now line the side of the room closest to the door, and a few of them are filled with men talking in loud, gruff voices. The sea painting hangs above them, the one thing in the room that hasn't been moved. Marie and her cart are against the wall opposite, and a few men grab some small bites of cake to nibble as they pass on their way to the table.

“I'm not ready for this,” Henry whispers as he leans in close. “They're all expecting me to lead them, and I'd rather run away.”

"Shhh," I say back. "You don't want them to know that."

"Right." He adjusts his shirt, tugging down on the front of it and smoothing it out. Then, taking two steps forward, a newfound confidence emanates from him as he opens his mouth and speaks so all can hear. "What have we come up with so far?"

One of the men at the table turns toward Henry. "Your highness, we think we have a plan."

"Show me then," Henry replies.

He points to the map behind the table, and I recognize it from my childhood. Father used to show it to me as he pointed out various important places in the region. To the north, on top of them all, stands my country, Cray, well over half its perimeter sea-bordered. In the center, nearly landlocked, lies Fallund. And to the south and west, a country I know little about. Tern.

Picking up a quill, the man dipped it in ink and then took it to the map, drawing a line partway across the Southern border of Fallund. "This is the land believed to be inhabited by the barbarians. This is where we believe Tern will attack. Straight on."

"So what's our plan?"

"Well, at first, we thought to stand back, allowing

them to slaughter the barbarians at will, and only acting in self defense if things came far enough into our country."

"And now?" Prince Henry asks. I watch him, his eyes fierce and determined as he listens to them.

"Sire," Bern says. "We seek his majesty's approval for any plan we decide on. If you do not like this plan, we want you to let us know."

"What is it?" Henry asks.

"Our plan..." began the first man. His long, scrawny, hosen covered legs stand out to me. I'd only ever noticed his nose before, when his legs had been tucked under the table. He looks to Bern momentarily, as if seeking approval before letting the prince in on their strategy. "Our plan is to come to this point." His finger falls on a speck of land very near their southern border.

"But that's nearly into Tern," Henry says. "What purpose will that serve?"

"We mean to communicate with the barbarians, seek an alliance with them—of sorts—and ensure that Tern stays within its border. If it's a war they want, a war we will give them."

Henry looks to me, but what can I do except shrug my ignorant shoulders, which I do.

"What are the risks?" Henry asks. I think it is a wise

question.

Bern answers him. “Tern's army is much larger than ours. Even with the barbarians fighting on our side, we may lose. Once this war is over, they may seek further battles, out of revenge. It could go on for ages.”

“Are there any other risks?”

Bern looks away, and I think he must not be ready to accept all the risks yet. The tall, thin man answers instead. “The barbarians may turn on us. It is unclear whether they know a war is coming or not. We know little about their communication abilities as it is. If we frighten them, we may start a war on our own, without any help from Tern. After that, they will come anyway, and the casualties on our side will be catastrophic.”

I watch Henry’s eyes twitch, and imagine he wants to cover them, or rub his forehead, or run his fingers through his hair, but he stands firm, his hands clasped behind his back. “Are there any advantages?”

“Yes, your majesty,” Bern says. “We keep the war farther away from our people. We teach Tern a lesson about attempting to threaten us into war, and it is possible we form an alliance with a people that frankly, we’ve needed to deal with for a long time, even before the death of the king and queen.”

I am nervous for Henry at the mention of his parents, thinking he may not want to think about that right now, but it does not seem to affect him. "When will the army be ready?"

"They are moving as we speak, forming a straight line across the countryside where they will begin their march toward the southern border at our command. If we want them to be on the move by tonight, we need to alert them within the next three hours."

Behind us, the door opens and Duke pops his head in momentarily. "Master Henry, the smithy is here to measure you for armor."

At this, the tall man looks shocked. "Prince Henry, what does he mean?"

"He means it is time for me to be fitted into my armor. Bern and I will deliver the message to the army. I accept your plan. We are going to war."

"But why go yourself, sire? Do you mean to fight in the war?"

"I cannot ask my people to fight if I am not willing to fight with them." I smile at him admiringly. For a moment, although they look nothing alike, he reminds me of Father.

"Your highness, I am strongly against it."

"Your opinion is noted. Bern already tried to talk me out of it to no avail."

" But what if you perish? What will happen to the kingdom?" I cringe at the thought, hoping I will not have to witness such a thing.

"In that case, Duncan will be made king. It's not that complicated," Henry says, no emotion in his voice, no hint that it would matter to him either way. I wonder about this Duncan, whom I keep hearing about but whom I have yet to meet. Suddenly I am aware of the deep silence all around me, and most of the men have their heads pointed toward the ground. Are they silent because they worry for their leader? Or is it because they fear if this leader is lost, there is no hope in the next?

"Please finalize all the details. I will report back here in promptly one hour. Please have a written war plan for me to sign and take with me to the commanders of the army."

"Yes, your majesty," the tall man says. Bern nods at Henry.

He turns to leave and I follow, caught up in thoughts of how I ever came to be here. Had I never been cursed, would Prince Henry and I ever have met? Would the old alliance between our two countries have been enough reason to form any sort of friendship, or even acquaintance? He says he remembers me from childhood, but I have no recollection. For a moment, I am grateful for my curse, for my permanent state of slumber, for my frequent envelopment in strange dreams, and for the simple fact it all led me here—with him.

We walk outside the council chamber and around a corner before he drops the strong façade. Placing his head against the stone wall he lets out a heavy sigh. "That's the hardest thing I've ever had to do."

"You did it well," I say. "I knew you would."

10
BEAST

Morning light, bright and undaunted, shone down on the corridors and alleys surrounding the castle, warming Duncan's back and arms. He stepped lightly, feeling carefree himself, the events of his previous visit to the prison girl lingering in his mind. The thought of her hair beneath his hands in particular rested on his consciousness, imprinted and permanent. Winning her trust, even in that small measure, had been more satisfying than any other feat, even beating Henry at horseback racing or fencing as he had once or twice in their growing years.

"Morning, Thomas." The man waited outside, resting against the prison wall, soaking up the rarity of unhindered sunshine.

"Good morning to you, Prince Duncan," he said.

"How is she today?"

"Why don't you see for yourself?" He smiled as if he carried some great secret, a good secret, and Duncan rushed inside only to find . . .

"Marie?" The castle maid stood inside the prison

cell with the girl, beaming as she looked toward the prince. "Marie, what are you doing here?"

Only then did Duncan catch sight of her, and it took several seconds of staring and thinking, thinking and staring, until he realized it truly was her.

The rags, ripped and torn, had vanished, replaced by a long dress, light brown with petite sleeves, and tied with a dark blue sash. An empty basin also stood inside the bars, and guessing by the luster of her hair and skin, as well as the fragrance of jasmine, she had bathed.

"Marie, what have you done?"

Thomas came and opened the cell door, allowing Marie to exit. As she passed through, she handed the hairbrush to Duncan and said, "Your turn. I've been brushing since dawn." A wide smile formed on her lips. When the prince gave no response, she tried to explain. "I thought a bath may entice her, when I heard of how much she loved you brushing her hair. My daughter Marguerite chose the dress." She looked to the girl, examining her work, glowing with pride. "There may be hope for her yet, as far as taming her goes."

Though pleased, Duncan couldn't help wondering what the purpose of taming her would be, if she was only to be killed anyway, and shortly. Her time was running out.

Thinking of this, Duncan turned to Thomas and whispered, "What is the trial looking like?"

"There are two witnesses," Thomas whispered in return. "But they are related to each other and the court may dismiss at least one testimony for that reason alone. It has happened before, when they believed the two related persons were plotting together. If another unrelated witness comes forward, that will be the end of it."

Duncan hated politics and law. Even that simple explanation had been enough for a life's worth. He turned to the maid. "Marie, how are her spirits? I mean, I can see she looks well, but do you have any idea what is going on inside her head? Or her heart? Has she spoken to you at all?"

Before Marie could formulate a response, an unexpected voice sounded. "Why do you ask your maid how I am feeling?"

"Did I mention she's been talking?" Marie asked, leaning in close and speaking so low Duncan was sure the girl could not hear.

"Thank you, Marie. I will take it from here."

"Would you like me to stay in here?" Thomas asked.

"No. Thank you, Thomas. You may see Marie outside."

Duncan waited until they left before speaking again. She stood tall, although perhaps a little insecure. Still, nothing like the crouched, hunched over figure he'd encountered that first day. Her teeth looked clean as well. The prince glanced to the floor and noticed an empty bowl of stew of some sort, and a plate with a thick, half eaten slice of bread.

Surprised, Duncan couldn't resist asking. "Did you eat stew?"

She smiled, and the prince couldn't remember ever seeing a lovelier sight, or a brighter grin.

"May I come in?" he asked, still feeling a little nervous that Thomas was not back to lock him inside. What if she tried to escape? What if she ran away and never came back? Taking one deep breath, he forced his mind to calm down and think positive thoughts.

"I would like that," she said.

Once inside the bars, an unsettling, awkward feeling emerged. What a strange place to be with such a beautiful young woman. Never before had she seemed more out of place, standing with grace, answering with a soft voice, and Duncan vowed once again to do whatever he could to help her.

After clearing his throat, Duncan asked if she would

like him to brush her hair.

"I would like that very much." She walked toward him and sat in the chair that had become a welcome piece of furniture, the *only* piece of furniture, in her small space.

Gently lifting a section of her dark golden hair, straight and flowing like a waterfall, Duncan continued what had begun with Marie. "So, how are you feeling? What do you think about in this dark prison cell all day?" Hoping he had not pressed too far, or not asked the wrong thing he waited for a response.

"I feel alone. And I think about all the things that have happened in my life. I recall them one by one, over and over. I think of nothing else."

Not sure if it was safe to ask another question, or try for more detail, Duncan waited, sending the bristles deep into her hair and moving them downward only to lift and repeat time and time again. Did she ever tire of this?

"What do *you* feel? What things do *you* think about?"

The questions took Duncan off guard. He had only wanted for her to express these things, not to spill open his mind and heart as well. But could he keep these things from her and still continue to earn her trust? Thinking it unwise to keep her waiting, he simply blurted the first things that came to his mind.

"I feel confused. At times I don't even want to be a prince. And I think about a lot of things, but mostly people, the merchants in the rows, the servants in the castle, my dead parents, my brother . . ." Should he say it? "You."

Seemingly unaffected, she sat motionless, all but her long hair, which Duncan continued to lift in his hands and brush through with the soft, thick bristles.

"How did you know I liked my hair to be brushed?"

"I didn't. Not until I tried it."

A loud bell pealed outside. The girl covered her ears, throwing her head sharply downward as the brush yanked out a few strands of hair.

Thomas ran inside. "Prince Duncan, have you heard? We're going to war. Today."

The worry on Thomas's face, followed by the sudden unrest outside the prison and around the corner on the rows, drew his attention away from the girl momentarily. He soon found that to be unwise. She leapt from her chair, ears still covered, an expression of terror on her face.

"You'd better get out of there," Thomas urged.

Not wanting to leave her alone, Duncan lingered, holding up his arms and trying to calm her by telling her that everything was all right. But it was too late. A low rumble came from her mouth, followed by a louder, more threatening yell. The prince escaped quickly, instructing Thomas to lock the door.

A man appearing in the doorway cast a shadow on the floor in front of Duncan.

"We are at war! They are looking for men to join the army to be trained and head out in a week. Prince Henry leaves today, along with the soldiers already trained. Prince Henry himself is going to war!" He ran off, as though he meant to shout the same message into every door along the rows and alleys.

Duncan looked to Thomas.

"It's not all bad news, sir. A war will delay her trial."

It sunk in, deep into Duncan's heart, the information about Henry going to war. Astounded by this, he ran for the door, leaving the girl behind, and his immediate concern for her, forcing his country and his family to the forefront. What could his brother be thinking? He could be killed. Duncan would be left completely alone, with no family left, a country to run on his own. He had to talk some sense into him.

Resenting the sunlight now, which caused sweat to pour from him by the time he reached the castle walls, Duncan stopped, thinking again of the girl. Her trial would be delayed. Formulating a plan, Duncan burst through the front castle doors. Things had been busier than usual lately, but he couldn't believe the sight before him. The castle often seemed nearly empty, with only the occasional interaction with servants, especially if one stayed toward the back of the castle, but people were everywhere, hustling about, a line of them coming from the tower stairs and continuing all the way up. Not commoners, as their father had allowed in his lifetime to wait in line and speak to him one on one, but merchants, aides and council men, dressed in finer clothing than the peasant class.

Duncan grabbed hold of someone's arm who passed him. "Where can I find Prince Henry?"

The man barely stopped, waving Duncan's hold on his arm away and continuing forward. "In the tailor room, being fitted for his armor."

Fitted for armor? So it was true. Henry would leave, go into battle with their country's trained soldiers. What did he know about fighting in a war?

Rushing up the stairs two by two, Prince Duncan found himself face to face with Henry in no time. He shoved the tailor room door open, taking in the sight of his brother standing up on a stool, breastplate hanging from his shoulders as a man measured and adjusted the silver armor around his right arm. A large mirror covered most of the far wall, granting Duncan a view of his own face as well.

"Hello Duncan," said Henry, instantly irritating the younger prince of Fallund. How could he be so calm at a moment like this? So practiced at indifference? "We missed you at the war meeting earlier. Did you get my letter?"

"Yes, I got your letter." Duncan breathed heavily, having been winded by the run from the prison and up the stairs. "And I told you. I am against this war."

Henry turned away, probably as a mock convenience to the tailor who had begun to move to his other arm.

"What do you think you're doing?" Duncan scolded.

"I'm getting ready for war."

"You're doing this on purpose. You mean to die, don't you? And escape your destiny to be king. It's too much pressure for you."

Remaining calm, Henry answered him. "How dare you say those things to me? You, who have done nothing but escape for the last five years?"

"Why, then?"

"To lead my people. To show them there is nothing to be afraid of."

Duncan spun around, turning from his brother in

frustration, briefly holding his forehead in his hands before facing him once more. "At least write to Cray then. Ask for their assistance. Ask them to restore the alliance."

"I can't do that. I won't."

"Why not? I demand you tell me."

"Very well then." Henry stepped down from the stool and removed his breastplate. "If you'll excuse us." Henry helped the tailor remove the armor around both arms and waited for him to exit.

After the tailor left the room, Duncan was left to anticipate a response for what felt like minutes.

"Listen to me," Henry said, walking toward his brother until they were close enough that Duncan felt the breath coming from his nostrils. "There is a reason that I cannot ask Cray for help."

"Well, what is it?"

"I am in love with the sleeping princess."

Duncan stared at his brother's face, his determined jaw, his wide cheekbones, his five freckles. "What did you say?"

Releasing a breath of air, as if agitated that he had to say it again, Henry repeated himself, every bit as quietly as before. "I am in love with the sleeping princess."

"In love?" This had been unexpected. Duncan had

heard the circulating rumors about Henry talking to himself, seeing ghosts, carrying on conversations with walls and hedges, but he hadn't believed there had been any grounds for such rumors. "In love . . . with the *sleeping princess*?"

Henry nodded, taking a finger up to his mouth and beginning to bite his nail.

"Henry, for the love of heaven and earth, what has gotten into you? She's asleep. You've never met her."

He lowered his hand and straightened his chest, but still carried a look of uncertainty. What was he so afraid of?

"Duncan, I don't expect you to believe me. But I'm going to tell you anyway. Eglantine, the cursed, sleeping princess of Cray visits me in her dreams. We talk. I can see her . . ."

"You can . . . *see* her?"

"Yes, and hear her."

Duncan nodded, searching his brain for a solution, wondering if going off to this war was really Henry's biggest problem right now.

"If I ask Cray to come to war with us, then her father will be in danger. King Bartholomew always fights alongside his soldiers."

"Is she the one who gave you this harebrained idea of going to war with the army?"

"No," Henry answered, as serious as Duncan had ever seen him. "I fight for my people. I go to lead them. She has nothing to do with that decision."

"She only prevents you from asking for help?"

At that, Henry shifted his focus, turning away from Duncan and facing toward one of the walls. "Shhh, Eglantine. I can't concentrate with your shouting."

Duncan looked around, half expecting to find someone with how unabashedly Henry had exclaimed his plea for silence.

"Is she here now?"

"So you believe me?"

"No, absolutely not." What an appalling idea, that Duncan would believe such inventions, such hallucinations, such witchcraft, if that's what it was.

Henry's face fell, taking a drastic change in mood. "I understand."

"Do you? Do you really know what's at stake here?"

"Yes, I know what's at stake. And the worst thing that could happen is that I die and leave your sorry, hesitant, irresponsible self to rule this country." Henry's eyes brightened, as if he'd just realized something. "Is that what you're really worried about? That I will die and you will have to take my place as heir to the throne?"

Duncan fisted his hands and clenched his jaw, but forced the air in and out of his nostrils in order to calm down. "You're a fool if you think the only thing I care about is myself." He couldn't be stopped now. He'd made up his mind. "And maybe I hate attending meetings that I think are pointless and fruitless, but I will not let my brother go into war alone."

"What are you talking about?"

"I plan to come with you."

Twisting around in a half circle, Duncan began to leave the room.

"Where are you going?" Henry called after him.

"I have to take care of something. Have the smithy adjust another set of armor for me."

Glancing back at the look of stupor on his brother's face, Duncan also saw something alarming. Henry began carrying on a conversation when there was nobody left in the room. So the rumors were true. Duncan had now witnessed it for himself. Going to war was a necessity, not only to protect his brother from the blows of weapons, but to protect him from his own insanity. If that could be done. Perhaps it was too late already.

Leaving these thoughts behind, Duncan headed for the prison once more, wanting to see the girl and explain that he would not be back to see her for some time.

Outside, Duncan thought how cruel it was that the sun would shine so hot on such a day. Darkness and gloom seemed more fitting for the prospects of war. As he walked, and was reminded of the commotion of earlier, and the bell ringing, he wondered if she had calmed down. Would he be saying goodbye to the beast or the beauty?

Thomas waited inside now, and Duncan didn't blame him for staying out of the sun's incessant heat.

"Is it true, Prince Duncan? Is Prince Henry going to war?"

"Yes, Thomas. It's true."

"I knew it. I think it's brave. What do you think?"

Duncan wanted to laugh, but couldn't quite let it out. "I think it's foolish. But you're right. It is also brave."

"She's been quiet since you left."

Duncan caught sight of her, walking about the cell as if lost.

"May I have a moment with her?"

"As you wish."

Thomas left and Duncan approached the bars, her wandering path remaining unaltered as she paced around and around in a circle.

"How are you feeling?" he asked.

Worried her silence meant regression, Duncan dropped his head and ran his fingers through his hair. At least she hadn't torn up her dress, or bitten anybody. Her hair still shined bright in the glowing rays of sun coming through the window.

"I came to tell you something. The kingdom is at war, and I will be going to fight in the army."

When she didn't appear alarmed, or affected whatsoever, Duncan continued. "I'm sure I'll be back in a few weeks, but I wanted to let you know that we may not see each other for a time." His heart beat faster, and a warmth spread through him. He didn't want to leave her. He may even stay if she asked him to. The thought of Henry and the sleeping princess came to mind, but Duncan couldn't understand why since he hadn't believed him. In love with the sleeping princess? Is that why Henry was acting so strange?

With his attention back on the prison girl, Duncan wondered if he could really be in love. Is this what love felt like? Troubled and scared by the thought, Duncan began to back away from her. "I'll miss you," he stated before turning to leave.

As he spun around, he nearly tripped and fell over someone. Bracing himself, and regaining his balance, he expected to see Thomas. Upon closer inspection however, Duncan discovered it was the old woman, the one who lingered around the prison and whom he suspected followed him on occasion, the one who had also entered his dreams.

Her moist, rosy lips moved slowly as she spoke. "If you leave she may not come back."

It sounded like a riddle.

Duncan squinted at her, hoping she would say more, but she turned around and slowly ascended the stairs, disappearing into the blinding glare of the sun.

11

Beauty

I am in and out of this war dream, weary from trying to manipulate where my dreams take me. I walk beside Henry's horse, having learned to imitate the act of moving my legs rather than floating or flying. I like being near him, though he is severely tense and does not talk to me much.

He argues with his brother again, and I wonder why he ever agreed to go in the same company with him.

I look over the vast countryside, the young wheat stalks waving in the breeze.

"We'll make camp once we reach the forest," Henry yells to Duncan and the other captains. I can see the forest from where we are, though it is a great distance off. It appears to be nothing more than a black line.

A smell catches my attention: orange blossom. Is Aunt Cornelia visiting me today? Are Mother and Father with her? I focus on Henry, his horse cantering beneath him. I will not leave him.

It takes three hours to reach the forest in our

formation, but in my state I am barely aware of the passage of time, only that the sun is nearly down. The men on horses dismount, and begin pulling down their packs and tying up their animals.

Henry pulls away from them, seeking solitude. I watch him bring the rope around a tall tree.

"How are you?" I ask him.

A heavy breath seeps out of his mouth. "They're tired, Eglantine. They're unprepared, their spirits low."

"They follow their leader."

He looks at me for the first time since we left our last camp early this morning. "Do you mean something by that?"

I ignore the accusation, refusing to give in to his attempt to pull me into an argument. Spending the last few days with him, I've learned that is a habit of his. "I mean exactly what I say. They follow their leader . You are tired. You are unprepared, your spirits low."

"I'm not cut out for this."

Duncan comes around a tree, a suspicious look on his face, as if he'd been spying on us, which to him would only mean Henry. I think of how he must really look crazy. He tries to only talk to me in secret, but he's been caught several times so far.

They take a long stare at each other until Duncan breaks the silence between them. "Some of the men are low on supplies, and request permission to hunt."

"What do you think is best?" Henry asks his brother in return. The question surprises me. Is he so tired that he can't make this simple decision?

It appears Duncan is surprised by the question as well; Henry has not asked his opinion on anything so far. "I think if we form a small hunting party it should be all right as long as we don't go too far and stay close together."

He is about to turn and leave, but stops. "Is she . . ." Duncan begins. His hesitation is like a sheet of thin ice over the water, and Henry dares not intrude upon it. We wait for Duncan to finish his sentence. "Are you still seeing her? Is that who you were talking to? The sleeping princess?"

Rather than answer, Henry begins setting up his bed and pulls a sack of supplies from the pouch strapped to his saddle—almonds and berries surrounding a small chunk of stale bread.

"Henry, I think you need some sleep. You've been guarding nearly every night."

Knowing this to be only a partial truth, I think of the nights previous. Henry had volunteered again and again, knowing I could watch for him and he could sleep, and not only that, but all the men around him could sleep also.

"Please don't tell me what to do. I don't need to sleep."

"Fair enough. I'll go out with the hunting party. Captain Storm says we should reach our final destination tomorrow before midday. Should we prepare a party to meet with the barbarians first thing?"

"That sounds like a good plan. You are far better at this than I am."

Duncan leans in close. "Henry, take heart. It will work out in the end. You will see."

Henry gives a half smile to his brother and nods as he sets out a thin wool cloth for his bed.

"He looks so much like you," I say, sitting next to him. "It's surreal, much like my dreams sometimes, like when I go to a place that I know I've been before, but it's not quite the same."

"We are nothing alike other than our faces."

"I don't think that's true."

"Who asked your opinion?"

It's hard to tell if he's joking. Part of me thinks he's serious. I know he is under pressure I have never known, but I am tired of his attitude. "You're the one who asked me to come with you. Would you like me to leave?"

"No!"

I want to laugh at him, and if I could I would pick a pine cone off the ground and throw it at him. He sounds so desperate. "You need to relax. Engage in some light conversation. Henry, you're entirely too serious."

"Eglantine, I'm sorry for bringing you."

"Do you regret asking me to come?"

"Not for my sake."

"Then say no more. I do not mind being here with you, even though you're such a pain." He almost smiles at that. Almost, but not quiet.

My mind travels back to the day we left, the day Duncan had interrupted his armor fitting, the day I'd learned that he . . .

"Eglantine, what do you think will come of us?"

Caught off guard, I'm unsure how to answer. Is he speaking of the two of us, or of his country?

"What do you mean?"

"If Duncan and I both die, what will happen to our people?"

I catch a whiff of orange blossom again. Perhaps Aunt Cornelia is saying goodbye, leaning over me and whispering something, but I push myself away from any awareness of her.

I look at Henry, so burdened right now, his eyes tired and heavy looking, his shoulders slumped as he hugs his knees to his chest.

"Don't you have laws in place in case of something like that?"

He looks surprised by the question, then as if he's deep in thought. "I don't know."

"Well, I'm sure you do. I'm sure your father and his parents before him had a plan of action in case of something just like this. It sounds like you have a lot to learn about your kingdom. It can't be done in five years. You were not prepared for this war. It came suddenly, and you are doing the best you can."

He takes in a deep breath, lifting his shoulders and looking up through the trees to the darkening sky. "I'm terrified of losing him. That's what I'm most afraid of now. That Duncan will die and I will live. I'd never forgive myself."

I reach out to him. It feels natural to do, even though I cannot brush my hand against his cheek as I want to. "Then let's make sure nothing happens to him."

"I wish I could feel your hand," he says, placing a fist to his cheek. It is getting too dark for me to see the color of his eyes, the details of his face, but I know he is keeping his eyes locked on mine. "I meant what I told Duncan in the tailor room before we left."

I've been waiting for days now for him to bring it up, wondering if I'd imagined the words, or if some other sleeping princess existed besides myself. "All I remember about that conversation is that you shushed me when I tried to stand up for myself."

I mean it as a joke, but Henry does not even crack a smile.

"Perhaps you should get some sleep before the hunting party comes back. Tomorrow is a big day."

"Do you remember when we met as children?"

The question surprises me. He has never mentioned it since that first day I saw him in my dreams. "No," I answer.

He leans back, resting his palms on the wool blanket and looking back at the sky. "Your mother and father had brought you to Fallund for a visit. You stayed a night in our castle."

"Did I? I remember some of our trips to Fallund a little, but not staying in the castle. And we met?"

"You must have been only three or four, but I was old enough to remember." He looks at me once more, still solemn. "I was taken with you even then. Your cheeks were pudgier, and your hair is a bit darker and not quite as curly. Now you appear much like a ghost to me, but your gray eyes are as piercing as they ever were. We played together all evening—you, Duncan and I."

I am not sure why this memory of his wells up such emotion in me. "Get some sleep," I say because I can't bear to hear anymore. I want to be strong for him. He agrees and lies down.

I wait near him, thinking of this tender memory, wishing I could run my fingers through his hair, until Duncan returns. I watch as the younger prince of Fallund places a slab of cooked meat near his brother, having used tree bark for a plate, and covering it with a giant leaf to help keep it warm. I do not have to look closely to see their mutual affection, despite how hard they try not to show it to each other.

Henry wakes, probably because of the smell. He eats, offering me a bite with a teasing smile on his face.

Duncan steps toward us once more. "The men are tired and want to sleep."

"Very well. I am awake, and will watch over our camp tonight."

"I could stay up with you."

"No!"

I shrink in discomfort at having watched the exchange, and Duncan huffs as he turns to leave.

"Why don't you let him help you?" I ask.

"He needs his sleep. They all do."

"What about you?"

"I've had my sleep. I'll be fine." I try not to smile, knowing he will fall asleep shortly after everyone else and I will be left to watch over the camp alone. Not that I mind; it's just amusing that he can't admit how tired he is.

"Will you keep watch with me? In case I fall asleep again?"

Grateful for the recognition, I answer, "Of course."

* * *

At first sign of dawn, when only a hint of a glow beckons from the horizon, I make a quick sweep over camp, flying clumsily at first, then gracefully. There is no sign of anything up ahead of the intended march. I float back down to Henry and crouch beside his ear.

"Time to wake up," I whisper.

He jolts up so quickly that had I been physically present, his head would have smashed into mine.

I can see his heart beating fast against his chest. He reaches for his canteen, dribbles some water onto his hand and splashes his face with it.

"Is anyone else awake yet?"

"No, not that I could tell."

"Thank you, Eglantine, for letting us all get the rest we so desperately need."

"Who are you talking to?" I spin around and Duncan is standing right over us.

"I wasn't talking."

"Don't lie to me. I heard you."

"All right. Fine." Henry looks up to his brother, still sitting on his makeshift bed. "I was talking to the sleeping princess. I slept like a baby all night knowing she could keep watch since she never stops sleeping. Is that what you wanted to hear?"

"You're going mad. Henry, I think the pressure of all this is too much for you. Let me take you back to the castle, get you cleaned up, feed you a real meal."

"What are you talking about? You haven't eaten a real meal in over five years. I know because I eat at the royal dining table alone."

"Well at least I don't talk to people who don't exist."

Henry glances at me. I try to give him a look of

reassurance. I don't mind Duncan's words. I don't blame him, knowing he can't see me.

"Can we just forget about this for now?" Henry asks. "Please?"

"Whatever you say." I can hear the hurt in his voice. Bowing his head, Duncan walks away, and Henry stares after him for a time.

"We need to get packed up. The sooner we get on with this day, the sooner it will all be over, one way or the other."

I walk beside Henry again, once camp is packed up, and we move slowly, waiting for the scouts to return and bring us word. It is not a welcome sight to see them on their horses, coming up from behind a hill in the distance, riding at full speed toward us and yelling words we can't quite make out yet.

"Halt!" Henry yells, and those nearest stop first, followed by every soldier I can see spread out on either side of us. They hold their spears pointing upward or their bows and arrow-filled quivers strapped to their backs.

I look at Henry, sitting up straight on his horse, so poised and seemingly unaffected.

Then we see them. The ravenous barbarians coming, their screams growing louder and larger as more and more of them rise over the hill and fall in masses toward us. They sweep the land, cover a straight line as far as I can see.

"What's happening?" Henry yells to one of the scouts when he is close enough to hear.

"They saw us coming and turned to chase us, the whole lot of them it seemed."

"How many?"

"At least five thousand."

Henry squints at the people bearing down on us. I begin to notice their ragged clothing, made of thin animal skins mostly, and then I realize it isn't just men. Women and children are in the throng, holding knives, spears and axes alongside their grown male counterparts. Only the men hold bows and I wonder why. Have they not trained the women to use them?

Duncan is riding toward us. "We can't kill women and children."

"Well they're going to kill us! Men, prepare yourselves."

In unison, each soldier readies their weapon of choice, some pointing spears, some grasping their bows, and others holding onto a sword with both hands. They stand crouched and ready.

"We charge on three!" Henry yells. I do not want to watch. He turns to me quickly, and quietly pleads. "Eglantine, please keep an eye on Duncan."

"Of course," I say.

"One! Two! Three! Charge!"

At first, it feels slow, the soldiers pulling out, but soon there is a thunderous noise as the horses and men pound their hooves and feet across the grassy valley.

A woman catches my attention, her hair matted and wild, standing away from her head like an angry wave of the sea. She holds an axe and runs screaming, so determined that she pulls away from the rest. I watch a soldier aim his bow at her, pull back his arrow, and shoot. She is the first to fall, but the others continue undeterred, as if they hadn't even noticed. Those behind her run around her body or jump over her.

Looking toward Duncan, I try to read him. Not as unbending as Henry, he is worried, tentative, hesitant. I watch him make the first slicing swings of his sword. He kills only men, and seems to grow braver with every kill, although the look on his face—one of disgust and horror—tells me he isn't pleased with his actions.

Henry rides brave, and rather than killing at will, he strategically looks for those who are about to harm one of his men, a skillful protector.

The battle rages on, the clanging of metal, the spilling of blood, and I hate watching.

Duncan is hit. I see him fold forward, and an arrow sticks out of his side. Henry has not noticed, and I am grateful. Moving to Duncan, I hover around him, prepared to yell for the only one who can hear me if needed. But it is too late; an arrow is aimed right at him.

"Duncan, get down," I yell, and as if he's heard me he slips off his horse, dropping his sword and landing in a pile on the grass.

I kneel beside him.

"Duncan, lie down."

He looks around. "Who said that?"

He can hear me! "Duncan, it's Eglantine. Lie down and pretend you are asleep. That way they will leave you alone."

I try to drown out the horrible screaming and cries of agony, the groaning and slaughter, and just focus on him.

"Trust me," I urge him. "Please, lie down and try to sleep."

Duncan looks around, trying to locate me, and then his eyes meet mine, or so it seems. "Eglantine?" he asks.

"Yes," I sputter, an unexpected joy bursting out of

me at the idea that he can see me too.

He rolls over slightly and rips the arrow from his side, stifling a scream.

"Shhhhhh."

Resting his head on the grass near me and closing his eyes, he asks if I will sing to him, tells me it will comfort him to hear something other than the sounds of war.

He almost begs.

Flustered, I pull a song from memory, the only song I remember, and begin, uncertain at first, but growing stronger. It bends and sways, this song of the ocean tide, and soon he is asleep, the grass staining red beneath him.

12
BEAST

A gnawing pain at Duncan's right side forced him awake. Surrounded by dense, moist fog, he could see nothing. Breathing led to sputtering coughs, which only sent a resonating sharp pain through his stomach.

What had happened? Duncan searched his memory. It came in flashes, the sight of the barbarians turning to fight them, the surprise arrow through his side from the back, the gruesome sounds of war, and finally, the face of the ghost girl. Eglantine. He had seen the sleeping princess. She had warned him when danger was near so he could fake dead, and then answering his pleas, had sung to him.

Torn between the warning in his head that tried to convince him he'd been dreaming—or worse, hallucinating—and the guilt tugging at his heart that he'd been so cruel to Henry, Duncan closed his eyes and rested once more. Moving in any direction caused his side to sear in pain. Duncan lay on his back, his legs bent and crossed beneath him, stiff and achy; moving them would be every bit as difficult as turning over. His hands and arms tingled, feeling weighty and numb. Only able to shift his head, Duncan looked to his side only to find a corpse: eyes wide, mouth open, a soldier from his country that he did not know. Forcing himself to look away, Duncan thought of nothing but his own survival. How was he going to get back home?

The fog sped along above and around him, opening up in places to expand his view of the valley around him and the forest in the distance. A far-off call sounded, barely audible, a human voice. Not knowing whether the voice was friend or foe, Duncan waited patiently, prepared to fake dead again.

The voice grew closer, calling out the same two syllables over and over.

Finally, it became clear. "Duuuun-caaaan!"

Opening his mouth, Duncan tried to call back, but stopped at the resulting sputtering and coughing.

"Duncan?" It was Henry's voice.

He could hear the footsteps now, boots tromping across the damp grass with determination.

"Duncan?

"Here," Duncan called. "I'm here."

When Henry's face appeared through the fog, Duncan wanted to leap up, but no part of his trunk or limbs approved.

"Stay there," Henry said. "I'll bring my horse."

Duncan didn't know why, but when Henry turned to leave, a sudden fear seized him. Terrified of being left alone, he called for his brother to come back.

"Eglantine, I found him."

Hearing her name eased him some, which he couldn't explain either. Rather than worry, Duncan began thinking how wonderful it was that Henry had come out unscathed. He could never have lived with the idea that Henry had died while he had not.

A horse appeared above Duncan's head, forcing Duncan to wonder if he was still falling unconscious now and then; it had come out of nowhere.

"Don't worry, Duncan. We'll get you back home and fix you up."

"Is she here?" Duncan asked. "Eglantine?"

"Can't you pick a better time to make fun of me? You must not be hurt that bad if you can still take a jab at your brother."

Cursing Henry's stubbornness, Duncan tried to find a way to explain it quickly in order to save his breath. Talking took so much energy, and the words came out with such great difficulty because of the pressure in his chest.

"I've seen her." Duncan paused to make a few attempts to draw air into his lungs. "She stayed with me. Sang to me."

Henry knelt by his brother now. "I'm glad you had the chance to meet her. She's the one who led me back to you. If you'll be quiet now, this isn't going to be pleasant."

Duncan cried out in pain as Henry reached down and hefted him up into his arms.

"What?" Henry asked. He must have been talking to Eglantine. "Oh, right."

"I'm going to set you on the horse, but Eglantine reminded me that covering your wound would be a good idea."

The saddle was cold, and Duncan thought it felt unnatural compared to the grassy valley floor. Duncan leaned forward, grabbing hold of the horse's mane, trying desperately to think of something other than the pain, but having little success. Henry's arms wrapped a cloth around him several times as he tied his middle up.

"Is that too snug?"

Unable to answer, Duncan closed his eyes and felt a bit of bloody drool seeping out of his mouth.

"Don't worry, Brother. We'll have you home soon. A carriage waits just on the other side of the forest."

Duncan did not look forward to being moved again, and somehow the bumping from the walking horse rocked him back to sleep.

* * *

Duncan blinked slowly until his eyes adjusted to the light and he could keep them open all the way. He'd been in this room often as a child, and instantly recognized the ceiling painted like the daytime sky: blue with puffy, white, silver outlined clouds. Smelling an array of herbs and feeling a steam on his face, Duncan looked about.

Close to the door, a woman's face stared back at him. Startled by her presence inside the castle, Duncan jerked to the side, knocking over a tray on the table beside him. When he looked again, she was gone, a fold of her black cloak the last thing to escape before the door closed behind her.

"Hello?" Duncan called. "Can anyone hear me?"

He examined the pain in his side, trying to determine if he could move without causing further damage or passing out again. Pulling back the tan linen sheet, Duncan discovered that a clean bed robe covered his body.

The tight wrapping around his middle hugged the pain in, causing a sense of security. It hurt, but not nearly so much as it had when Henry found him. How long had it been?

A woman in maid uniform came through the door, but Duncan didn't recognize her.

"You're awake."

"Yes, thank you." Sitting up ever so slightly and resting on his elbow, Duncan sought to get some answers. "Excuse me, a woman just left here, an older woman. Can you tell me, what was she here for?"

"I've been the only one in today, sire. I've checked on you every half hour."

"No, that's not possible. I saw a woman leave only a moment ago."

A look of confusion came first, then worry. "I'm sorry, Master Duncan. I did not mean to let anybody in."

"Pay no mind." Duncan hadn't meant to alarm her, nor blame her. "Please come in. Please, tell me what day it is. What has happened? Where is my brother?"

Looking even more troubled, the woman began asking her own questions. "Would you like me to tell you what I know or would you rather me get Prince Henry first."

"No, no, I'm sorry. Tell me, what is your name?"

"Marguerite."

"Marguerite? Are you Marie's daughter?"

"Yes, your majesty. How did you know?"

"You picked out the dress. The one for the prison girl. I remember. Your mother is very proud of you."

"Yes, sire." She lingered by the door, as if hesitant to enter. "Would you like me to get Prince Henry?"

Yes, talking to Henry would be better. "That would be much desired. Thank you."

"You're welcome, your majesty." She bowed her head before retreating out the door.

Only a few minutes went by before Henry came in. A broad smile graced his face, but it soon turned to a solemn stare. "I see you're awake. And determined to interrupt another council meeting."

"Really? You were just in a meeting?"

Henry nodded, his face stern.

"My timing really is bad."

Walking toward his brother, Henry's seriousness broke. "Yes, well, it always has been, and I don't expect that to change." He sat on the side of the sick bed, smiling once more. "I'm glad you're awake."

"So am I." Sitting up a little more, Duncan felt a sharp pain cut through his middle. "I think."

"Are you all right?"

"Thanks to you . . . I will be."

"You can thank Eglantine."

"Is she here too?"

"She never leaves. It's becoming quite obnoxious. Okay, okay, I'm sorry."

Duncan could see a change in his brother, a ray of hope or joy shining through his eyes. Had it come because of the end of the war? Or was it the girl?

"What happened, Henry?"

"Do you remember when you told me you hated my idea about going to war?"

"Which one? I hated them all." Trying not to laugh because it hurt too much, Duncan placed his right arm across his middle, determined to hold it still even if a laugh did slip out.

"Well, your plan is sort of what happened anyway. On accident. When we arrived, the Tern had already attacked. Fearing we were attacking from their rear, the barbarians turned on us before we ever had the chance to talk of peace. It was a great slaughter, on all sides. But once we cut through the barbarians and reached the Tern, we called a halt. They believed we had come to their aid and met us with joy. Victory."

"What about all those women and children?"

"Many were spared, and are being given designated land in Fallund territory as part of the peace agreement."

Thoughts of the prison girl came to mind. These were her people. How would she take the news? Or had she been glad to escape them?

"Henry, how long have I been asleep?"

"Not as long as Eglantine." He chuckled at his own joke.

"Will you thank her for me?"

"Why don't you thank her yourself? She's standing right next to me."

Duncan looked to the side of his brother and up a little, not knowing exactly where she would be or how tall she was. "Thank you." Turning his focus again to his brother, Duncan began to plead. "Henry, please. Give me a straight answer. How long have I been asleep? What has happened to the girl?"

A dark look fell upon Henry, a solemnity that Duncan found alarming and unwelcome. "Henry, what has happened?"

"A third witness came forward. Her trial is over. She awaits execution. You've been asleep for a week."

The pain in his side seemed nothing now, not compared to the oppressive ache in his heart. He had failed her.

"There is one more thing you missed while sleeping. A coronation. I am now *King* Henry."

This was welcome news, but overshadowed by the heaviness layered on top of Duncan's chest. "I want to see her."

"She's in isolation. Not only is that the law, but she's worse than ever, a danger to anyone who comes near."

Duncan glared at his brother, determined to win this battle before it even began. "You're the king. Pull some strings. I want to see her today."

* * *

Duncan and Henry walked along an Eastern Row.

"I don't see how you like wandering around outside the castle so much. It's dusty, and the people are so . . ."

"So what? These are your people, Henry. This is what normal people actually dress and sound and act like. Not one of them has had your privileges. And not one of them deserves your censure, nor your judgment. Besides, you get used to it after a while."

"I'm sorry, Duncan. I didn't mean to upset you." He

turned to his other side. "Or you, Eglantine."

Duncan had forgotten that Eglantine was near. She was good for Henry.

Rounding the corner of Northeast Alley, Duncan saw the woman once more, bending over a basket as she picked at the things inside, her long black hair almost touching the ground.

"There she is." Duncan watched her arranging things in her basket until she looked straight at him.

"Who?"

"The woman who was in the sick room today."

Henry pointed. "That woman there? She was in the castle? Well, that seems unlikely."

She began walking toward them, slowly, but definitely directly toward them.

"What?" Henry was talking to Eglantine again. For a brief moment, Duncan thought of how comical it was to see him talking to her. "Are you sure?" He turned to his brother. "She says it's the witch who cursed her."

"Eglantine?"

"Yes."

Could it be? The old woman who followed him was actually a witch? The same witch who had cursed Eglantine all those years ago in the kingdom of Cray. What did she want with him? Hadn't their father seen to the death of all the witches?

"It's all right, Eglantine. She can't see you." Turning to Duncan again he adds, "She's hysterical. She says the witch can always see her."

"She's not looking at Eglantine. She's looking at me." The old woman continued forward until she stood in front of Duncan.

Her slow voice, her dark hair and tall, slender form, her black cloak, everything about her now seemed more ominous, more threatening. "I told you that if you left she may not come back."

The riddle again. Whom was she referring to?

Slowly she rounded Duncan and began to walk away, bumping him with her basket as she did so.

"See there?" Henry spoke to Eglantine again. "Everything is just fine." Then calling to his brother said, "Duncan, I'm going to stay out here with Eglantine. We may even head back to the castle. Will you be all right?"

"I'm sure I will."

Phillip, one of the prison guards, let the prince come in, and having received word earlier in a letter stamped by the king, showed Duncan to the isolation cell. Passing by the bars of where the girl had stayed previously, where Duncan had first helped to place her, and where he'd brushed her hair and seen her standing in the bright sunshine and simple dress, caused an inexplicable nostalgia. If only she were still in there; the isolation cell meant her fate was sealed. A wooden door led to a narrow hallway which led to another wooden door. "We've been given orders not to open it until execution day. We only feed her through there." He pointed to a slot near the bottom of the door.

A quick internal debate about whether to open it or not was put to rest when a loud slam rattled the door in conjunction with a horrifying scream.

Torn apart even further, Duncan sagged his head. What had he done?

"You may leave me here, Phillip. I'll try to talk with her through the door."

Another slam startled the guard before he turned and left.

Duncan waited a moment, blocked from any idea of what he might say. He leaned against the door just in time to feel it slammed again. The weight thundered beneath his chest, agitating the sore spot on his side.

"Hello?" he called.

A heart wrenching scream tore through the air,

echoing loudly and tormenting the prince.

Duncan waited for the screaming to stop. "Hello?"

No slamming against the door, no blood curdling screams came from the other side, but no acknowledgement or civil response came either. "It's me. Prince Duncan. Did I ever tell you I was a prince? No, I don't think I did." The sound of his own voice echoing through the hallway in a one-sided conversation left Duncan feeling like he was the only person in existence. "Please answer me."

Disappointed, but grateful for the current calm, Duncan continued. "I want you to know that I'm sorry for not coming for so long. I missed seeing you . . . and combing your hair. And I'm sorry about . . ." Duncan couldn't think of a way to say it delicately. "I'm sorry I couldn't do more to help you." Was he really going to give up that easily? *Could* something else be done?

The door opened and Phillip poked his head inside. "Is everything all right, Prince Duncan?"

"Yes, Phillip. Everything's fine. I'll just finish up and be out in a minute."

After the guard left, Duncan tried to think of what the best thing to say would be, the thing that would be most likely to get her attention. He wasn't ready to say goodbye.

"Do you mind if I keep coming to see you?"

He knew she could answer. He knew she was in there, listening to his words. "Will you please find a way to let me know if that is satisfactory to you?" Resting his head against the door, he wanted to beg. "Please? Will you knock once if you never want me to come back, and two times if you would welcome me again?"

The silence cut through the air, louder to Duncan's heart than any bell, no matter how close to the ear it rang.

Then a knock sounded, which at first sent a shock of trepidation through him. Would she stop after one knock?

Then another. Duncan let out a sigh of relief, and allowed a little smile to form on his lips, and a little hope to enter into his soul.

Now he could say it. "Goodbye."

After both speaking and waving a goodbye to Phillip, Duncan went outside, breathing in the cool air. He imagined dusk riding in slowly, as if on a distant carriage, the sun low, the colors dampening.

As he walked, around the corner came the woman again. Determined to say something to her, to get some answers, Duncan approached her.

To his surprise, before he could open his mouth,

she spoke first. "She is still in there."

Duncan wondered whom she was referring to. The fact that she had cursed Eglantine, that she sneaked about the corridors and alleys surrounding the castle, that she never seemed to leave, frightened him, and more than anything, he wished she would spill whatever secrets she seemed to be holding fast. "Do you mean the girl in the prison?"

"I am not talking about the beast inside the prison walls. I am talking about the girl inside the beast."

Riddles again. Duncan had never been good at riddles. "Do you know her?"

"I do. And she used to know me."

"Who is she?"

"She is my child, or was, long ago."

"What happened to her?"

"Too many things."

Feeling more urgent now, wanting to get as much information as he could while she answered him freely, Duncan took a small step forward, leaning low to her and asked, "Do you know of Eglantine, the sleeping princess from Cray?"

"The sleeping princess is no concern of mine."

"Are you the witch who cursed her?" Fearful this

question might bring adverse reactions, Duncan took a step back, pulling away from her.

"The sleeping princess is no concern of mine."

Squinting, Duncan tried to understand, frustrated that she gave insufficient answers most of the time. He felt certain she kept some secret. The woman began to walk around him. Determining that meant she had finished engaging in conversation, Duncan began a slow, thoughtful walk back to the castle, only to be interrupted almost instantly.

"Would you like to know her name?" The voice had come from close behind, and Duncan jerked around, startled. There she stood again, facing him as before, only their positions had changed.

"Yes. I would like to know her name."

"Ovinia, although she will not recognize it."

The woman—the witch, if that's what she was—turned around and walked down Northeast Alley, her floral dress and cloak sweeping up a cloud of dust as she left. Duncan watched her until she turned onto one of the Northern Rows, and vanished from sight.

13

Beauty

Henry sleeps, his breaths small and light, one arm stretched out long underneath his head, the sheets on his bed covering all of his lower body except one knee. I stand near the window, watching the night sky—with the moon low, fist-shaped and bright—and the quiet outside world standing as though it is a statue, or a painting.

As I think of home, and my own bedroom in my own castle far away, a biting homesickness prickles every fiber of my being. I long to see my parents, Aunt Cornelia, the ocean. I imagine it now; closing my eyes I picture the sound of it, the rushing and swaying, the waves running in to greet me only to sink back again. It is the game that we play. Standing in my room, five years old, I run to the window to greet the waves, then step backward in goodbye.

Her dark eyes haunt me, the witch who cursed me all those years ago, walking in daylight and freedom through Fallund, while I am trapped in a world known only to me, a world I cannot even completely share with Henry because I am not *actually* here.

It is a gloomy night, though the skies are clear and the air is calm and brisk and cool. At least, that is how it feels to me. But is it the air in Fallund that I breathe, or the air in Cray by the seaside? I reach out my hand to touch the window pane, but feel nothing.

I am nothing.

I never used to feel such despair. Sorrow perhaps, and a desperate yearning to see my parents again, but never this despair and hopelessness I feel now. I know it is because of him.

I watch him now, his mouth open, his pillow hugged tightly to his chest in one arm, and I understand why I feel such pain. He loves me. And I have grown to love him, but I remain asleep, living a curse that I never deserved. By the time my mother gives birth to a boy, and he has a chance to grow old enough to free any beasts, Henry will be much older. I will be older as well, but it feels as though he will keep moving on and I will not. I wonder if Henry knows all the circumstances of the curse, the requirements of my freedom.

Weary of this dream, I try to catch a glimpse of my garden home, the glasshouse where I sleep. A whisper from Stella, a smell of lavender or lily, any of these would be welcome now. Being asleep while everyone else is awake is a lonely existence, but no more than being awake while everyone else is asleep.

Tonight, Henry and Duncan will host a ball to celebrate the war victory. Henry has begged me to come, but I'm not sure I want to. Watching him dance with women whose hands he can hold, who will be dressed in elegant gowns and bring curl-framed faces, while I stand pretending that I cannot see seems like torture rather than entertainment. I had a taste of this at the coronation, and I hated it. I never want to go through it again.

It is coming, the first glow of light. I watch the sky, the subtle, slow creeping of dawn, easing the world into a new day. Unable to take my eyes off it because I have missed so many sunrises, I do not hear Henry stirring and waking.

When the rounded tip of the sun peeks over the horizon, I turn to find him watching me as he sits on his bed.

"Did you sleep well?"

He rubs his eyes and yawns while nodding his head. I smile at the sight of him, the raw, weakened human being showing instead of the strong and steady king.

"What has got you looking so serious and

contemplative?" he asks as his hands grip the bed on either side of him.

I turn away from him, looking once more to the outer world. "I can't see my reflection. Not here in the window, nor in any of the mirrors throughout the castle." He remains silent so I continue. "Sometimes I dream I am standing over myself, and it is as though I am looking down on a statue. I imagine my skin hardening to white stone that will crack and chip away over time, my eyelids never to open. The garden vines climb all around me, suffocating me until I disappear into them, never to return." I turn toward him again, trying to keep the choking sensation in my throat at bay. I force a smile, but a tear slips from my eye. "I can't decide which is worse, the absence of my reflection in your window, or the statue dream."

"Eglantine, will you dance with me tonight?"

I scoff at the idea, telling him I'd rather sleep for another hundred years than make him look like such a fool.

He stands and makes his way to me, so close that I would be able to feel his breath on me if I could feel anything at all. "Take heart, Eglantine. All will be well. Will you excuse me while I get ready for the council meeting?"

I keep forgetting to tell him that he holds far too many meetings. I agree and tell him that I'll be waiting in the council chamber.

Rather than go straight there, I stop by the kitchen, aiming to catch the smell of fresh bread. I stop at the door and suck the air forcefully through my nostrils. I try a second time, but it is no use; I smell nothing.

Walking back up the tower stairs, I think of all the good foods I used to eat: ham and potatoes, jam spread over soft, hot bread, chicken soup and roast goose. I know Stella feeds me, or at least tries to force juice down my throat, but eating is one of the things I miss most, the texture of an apple on my lips, its sweet taste on my tongue.

Henry is already in the council chamber. "Did you get lost?" he asks when I enter, looking up from the parchments scattered on the table before him. "I was worried about you."

"I'm just hungry and stopped by the kitchen in the hopes . . ." I stop, thinking how foolish it was.

"I'm sorry, Eglantine. I wish I could give you something."

I shrug my shoulders, fighting back tears.

"Are you all right? Are you still thinking about the witch?"

He had given me so much comfort in the days before since I'd seen her—nearly encountered her—and I remembered his words. "She can't hurt you anymore. The worst is over," he had said.

I struggled to believe him wholly, but I allowed them to comfort me anyway.

Men began to come in now. He grins toothlessly at me, and I nod my understanding. He won't be able to talk to me, not until after the meeting. I find a wall to stand in front of, and begin to agonize over the coming evening.

* * *

Waiting outside Henry's room, I sweat uncontrollably. I know the sweat is real and not imagined because I am sticky with moisture. Hoping Stella does not give me tonic, I try to relax, try not to fidget so obviously. But how can I fool anyone if I cannot even fool myself?

I jump at the sound of his opening door, a rush of emotion pouring through me as I realize it is time to go. He is wearing a white shirt, covered in a sea green jerkin that brightens the color of his eyes, and dark gray velvet breeches tucked into black leather boots.

Frowning at my nightgown, I see his hand rising to touch my face, and for a moment I expect that it will. But deep down I know that his hand cannot touch my face, no matter how much he tries.

"You look beautiful," he says. "As always."

We walk together, down the tower steps as the din of mingling voices reaches my ears. We stop at the bottom step, where he is announced by his faithful servant Duke.

"King Henry, seventeenth king of Fallund, Captain of war."

He whispers to Duke, who afterward returns a strange look.

Then I hear my name, loud for all to hear. "Princess Eglantine of Cray."

Henry moves forward with confidence, but I am preoccupied by the people now staring at him and looking around for a mysterious princess from their neighboring kingdom.

"Pay no mind," he whispers to me.

We walk through the double ballroom doors and the music greets us with joviality as at least a dozen couples already swoop and sway across the floor. Browsing the room for a corner I can tuck away in, I get a glimpse of Duncan, already dancing with a pretty young woman dressed in a dark maroon gown.

"May I have this dance?" Henry asks. I turn to him,

surprised that he is already asking someone to dance until I realize he is holding his hand out to me.

"Are you crazy? You will look like a fool."

"I don't care what I look like, or what they think of me. Not as long as you are beside me."

I still think it unwise, and deep down am against it, but I cannot refuse his outstretched hand, not in this room full of people who do not see me reach out to accept it.

He leads me across the floor, twirling in a three-quarter turn, and back the other way in a slow one-two. I stare into his eyes, as he does into mine, incapable of keeping from smiling as he does so skillfully.

"You dance pretty well," he says. "For a lady who floats."

Even with that his lips remain in a steady line, and I wish I could hold my feelings back as well as he does. Perhaps I could if I was putting on a show for those around me. But since I know they are unaware of me in my nightgown, slippers and rumpled hair, I laugh out loud at his joke.

"Your smile could light up this whole room. If only they could see it." He had whispered this close to me, not teasing this time, but unfeigned in the delivery of his words, and I lean in closer to him, wishing I could feel him there.

We dance in continual motion, never stopping or pausing, no matter how the song changes or who we pass. I imagine them watching us, pretend they can see me, and that I wear an elegant silk gown, dark blue like the sea at night—no, light blue, like the sky on a brilliant, sun-sparkled day. They smile and whisper to each other of how lovely we look together, how well we dance, how perfect a match between the king of Fallund and the princess of Cray would be. All the while, Henry keeps his eyes fast on mine, his lips straight, his arms stiff in place as if they actually hold me close to him.

I don't know how many songs we dance through. I have not been counting, but Duncan walks toward us now, a look of determination on his face. He taps Henry on the shoulder, breaking the rhythm I cherish and do not want to let go of.

"Henry, what are you doing?" he asks.

Torn from watching Henry's face, I look around us. The people are smiling as I had imagined, and whispering, but it does not seem admiring. Mocking, perhaps, and definitely in wonderment, but not in admiration. I hear one woman whisper close by. "Who is he dancing with? I had heard he was losing his mind." She sounds pleased to be witnessing the evidence now. I notice for the first time that the music is gone. How long ago did it stop?

Duncan leans close to his brother's ear, and I listen to the words that come out. "Henry, I know you want to dance with Eglantine, but people are watching. You are their king. The room is filled with real ladies, young and old, who seek an opportunity to dance with their king."

The words push and prod at all my insecurities. A sense of shame encompasses me, and I suddenly feel exposed, standing in the middle of this ballroom in my white nightgown. Duncan considers me unreal; somehow this hurts the most, probably because it confirms my earlier fears, that Henry and I together simply will not work.

Henry searches my face, looking concerned. "I'm sorry," he whispers. "I understand if you want to leave." At that, he walks away from me, stepping up to the closest available "real" lady in the room and asking her to dance.

Tears flow freely now. Not only can I feel my cheeks getting wet, but I can taste the salt in my mouth. Somehow, I think Duncan will find a way to apologize, to locate my presence in this crowd of people, but he walks away too, as if I didn't even exist.

An unbearable heat fills my chest, a discomfort so foreign I can think of nothing else but to run. As I reach the edge of the ballroom, and pass through the double doors, I hear Henry's voice calling. "Eglantine!" But I know it is better if I leave. Better for him. Far better for me.

Night falls upon me as I run straight through the castle walls: the stillness and darkness hitting all at once as the voices and music stop instantly and I hear nothing but the chirping of crickets and the distant rumble of a carriage. I am in the garden, near the row of hedges where Henry and I used to meet.

It isn't long before he finds me. I turn to see him shoving through the back exit, breathless and a little rumpled—his hair tossed about and the top button of his jerkin undone. "Eglangine." That is all he can say before needing several more breaths.

I look away from him and up to the sky as I hug my arms around my shoulders. I think I must really be doing so in my sleep, for I feel the pressure of my hands against both my arms. It is comforting to be held by someone, even if it is only myself.

Henry walks through the grass and sits on the bench near me. I see no use in pretending to sit by him, so I remain where I am, probably floating above the ground, looking up at the bright starry sky.

"Eglantine, I'm sorry. Perhaps this whole thing was a bad idea."

"There's no need to apologize, Henry. You don't owe me anything. I don't expect you to stop living your life for me."

"How can you say that I don't owe you anything? I feel as though I owe you everything." I listen to him without looking, but imagine the expression on his face, his brow furrowed, his lips not only straight, but quivering. "Have you forgotten how you stayed here for me? Because I asked you to? How you came to war, watched over me, my brother, and the entire army? That you led me back to Duncan which probably saved his life? How can you say that I don't owe you anything?"

"I guess I don't see it like that." I hold on tighter, squeezing in, a cold shiver running up my spine.

"How do you see it then? Please, tell me."

Unwilling at first to confide such secrets, the desperate and regretful feelings of my heart, I simply breathe in the night air, trying to ignore the fact that the salty sea comes along with it, a reminder that while my mind is here, my body is elsewhere.

"I see a king who is destined for greatness. One with the grace to earn the respect of his people, and the hard work to ensure the success of his kingdom. And attached to his side, is a tumor, a growth that threatens to bring him down, one that is always in the way, and one that is easily removed."

"Your removal would not be easy, Eglantine, nor welcome."

I turn to him, pleading now. "It *would* be easy. I could slip back to my home, to my bed where I rest, and you would be free to dance at balls and attend meetings undisturbed."

"What makes you think that would be easy for me? It would be no easier than having my heart removed, and no less damaging. Eglantine, I don't keep you here for your own sake." He bows his head for a moment, then meets my eyes again. "I understand if you do not want to stay here with me, but I need you to know that I *want* you here."

"What if I never wake up? What if the spell is never broken?"

A loud crashing sound shatters the intimacy of our conversation.

Henry stands up, walking down the garden path toward the end of the castle grounds. I follow him and once we reach the final hedge, we can see around the castle. A cloud of smoke rises from a window on the main floor. As we stare, a fire bursts through, the fierce flames reaching up toward the sky.

"We need to get all those people out of the castle." Henry runs, but I know I am of no use to all those who cannot see me. I know the fire will not affect me; I will not feel the heat, nor will my skin burn. I can access things from the front end.

Henry is already out of sight when I enter the castle wall, near where the window had just burst to pieces. It is in the kitchen, and the flames are busy consuming a row of cupboards, and moving swiftly toward the doorway, threatening the rest of the castle. I plan to wait outside the kitchen for Henry, knowing he will be back once the people are to safety. That way I can let him know what the damage is and help keep him and anyone else away from the fire. The kitchen seems to have been empty, but as I move into the hallway outside, I see the back of her, the old woman from outside the prison, the witch who haunts me. Wondering if she is after me now, if she knows of my presence here and seeks to destroy this new home I have found, I follow her, a bitter and fluid anger pressing from the inside of me, begging to be unleashed.

I watch her round a corner and vanish from sight, and before I can catch up, Henry runs toward me. He is sweaty and breathless again, and Duncan is beside him.

"Eglantine, how bad is it?"

"It was her! The witch who cursed me started the fire!"

I am frantic, struggling to fight the urge to go after her.

"Eglantine, listen to me. She cannot hurt you. I need you to tell me how bad it is."

I nod repeatedly, uncontrollably.

"Henry, we've got to do something. Please forget about Eglantine long enough to put out this fire."

Determined to defy Duncan's lack of faith, and vowing to smack him if I ever meet him in person, I snap out of my hysterics, though I'm still shaking. "It's localized to the kitchen for now. I will keep watch. It was moving fastest toward the ballroom." My voice falters as I speak.

"Thank you, Eglantine."

"I'll keep watching."

Henry and Duncan, now surrounded by a host of men holding buckets filled to the top, set up a line so that water can be brought straight from the well outside in a continuous passage.

I keep watch over the fire until the last ember is splashed out, all the while thinking of her—the witch—not able to understand why she hates me.

14

BEAST

The aging night waited patiently for the newborn day. Exhausted, Duncan wiped his forehead only to find it grimy with sweat and ash. Cleaning up could wait; he had to find her tonight. He'd left Henry to organize the clean-up of the castle. They planned to work through the night. Duncan's job was to find the old woman, find her and question her.

Rounding the corner of Northeast Alley, Duncan learned that finding her would be the easy part.

"I knew you'd come," she said, a gloating look about her face as she rested her back against the outside prison wall.

"Was it you? Did you start the fire in the castle?"

He saw the admittance in her eyes. "Why?" Duncan was sincerely trying to understand, to get past the riddles and the secrecy and find out what she truly wanted.

The woman stood tall and began spitting accusations. "How can you smile and dance, and entertain ignorant, pampered guests while she is in there, getting closer and closer to her death with every passing day?"

It wasn't difficult for Duncan to admit to himself that he agreed with her. He hated that he'd been at a ball, dancing and pretending while . . . what was her name? Ovinia. Ovinia rotted in a cell, probably hungry and cold, definitely alone. Going to the ball had been more for Henry's sake. He wondered how the rest of the conversation would go, and suddenly his aim was not to blame, not to accuse, not to seek justice for the damage of the fire, but to hear whatever she would tell him.

"Why are you here?"

"To tell you her story."

"Does this have to do with the sleeping princess?"

She moved away from the wall and faced him. "I told you before. The sleeping princess is no concern of mine."

Duncan did not believe any more that Eglantine had nothing to do with the girl in the prison.

"Perhaps she is no concern of yours now, but was she ever? Does Ovinia's story involve the sleeping princess at all."

Her eyes blinked and her mouth twitched before she bowed her head and answered, "Yes. They were born on the same day."

"Is this their only tie?"

"It was until I cursed Eglantine. Now they are tied together through the curse."

"Why did you curse her?"

She began to walk, and Duncan fell into step beside her, the folds of her skirt brushing against his leg from time to time. "Ovinia was my first child . . . my only child. And I loved her dearly."

"What happened?"

"She was taken from me."

Duncan knew the answer to his next question before he asked; his father had spearheaded a movement to remove children from their witchcraft practicing parents. It had gone on long enough that Duncan remembered a few stories from his early childhood. Stolen children, hangings, paranoia and alarm. At one point, his father and mother had been so fearful of being cursed, that they left the kingdom for months. Upon their return, the king seemed to have given up the fight, and no longer meddled with the offspring of witches. But apparently, the damage had already been done in the case of Ovinia.

"Because you are a witch?"

She nodded, and seemed to pull away a little, as if she still feared what royalty in this country might do to her.

"Why did you curse Eglantine?"

"I fled to Cray, escaping execution, vowing that I would punish the king of Fallund, punish him by cursing his children. I knew, as a mother, that hurting his children was the most effective method of torturing him. When I knew your family was coming to Eglantine's fifth birthday party, I planned to attack. I had practiced cursing for years, giving up my gift of foresight for greater powers. Darker powers."

Duncan was beginning to see, piecing it together. "But we weren't there. Henry and I had come down with a fever, and we had to cancel our plans to visit Cray for the celebration."

"Yes. I didn't know that until after it was too late. When I burst into the dining hall that evening, fierce and determined, I first realized that the royal family of Fallund was not present. And then I looked upon her, that beautiful, healthy little girl, the exact age as my own sweet daughter, happy and loved. I took all my rage and forced it upon her, speaking a curse that I did not realize would be so impossible to break."

"And what happened to Ovinia?"

"After she was taken from me as an infant, Ovinia was placed with a family in the Southern country, a poor family, two brothers—one of which was married—who took her only for the slave she would one day become. The men abused her, often with the woman looking on and doing nothing to protect her, and several years after I had gone to Cray and cursed Eglantine, she left her home by night, and wandered into the land of the barbarians, where she learned their cold and cruel ways, fending for herself. Out of slavery, but into a world of brutality."

"And how did she end up here?"

"The men who she had lived with, they traveled too far into the southern woods one day, and seeing them, Ovinia took their lives into her hands, tormented by all those years they'd robbed her of her innocence and childhood."

"She killed them both?"

"Yes, but the witnesses only saw the one. She has only been sentenced for one."

"And you saw all of it?"

"Foresaw. I knew about all of it before I cursed Eglantine."

"What do you plan to do now?"

"If I'd known I was planting an impossible curse, I never would have bothered. The queen of Cray has been barren all these years, until recently I've heard. But by the time a son would come of age, Ovinia will be gone. The curse that ties her to Eglantine's freedom will be void. Only a brother can wake her by setting a terrible beast free. Ovinia was the beast I was speaking of. But you are her only hope now. Otherwise it will be too late."

"Why me?"

She stopped, turning and lifting her head to the prince—the slight wrinkles and crevices in her face barely visible in the moonlight. "Because you care."

"But what can be done now?"

"What are you willing to do?"

She started to walk again, but Duncan got the feeling she was walking away, that she didn't mean for him to come with her this time.

He called after her. "What about Eglantine?"

Holding up a hand in the air, as if waving him off, her back still toward him, she called back, "The sleeping princess is no concern of mine." Then she stopped, turning to face him. "I am sorry for what I've done to Eglantine. But I'm afraid she is trapped in her sleeping curse." She hesitated a moment. "Forever."

After watching her walk out of sight, her black cloak barely visible in the dark, Duncan made his way down the prison steps, pondering her last question. What *was* he willing to do? And Eglantine? Henry would be heart broken.

Thomas lay on the guard's bed, sleeping in silence. Rather than wake him, Duncan untied his keys from the rope around his waste, wondering what, if anything, he could actually do. What had the aging woman meant? Did she want Duncan to ease her last days? Or was she so foolishly hopeful to assume he would try to help her avoid punishment. Princes had little influence over trials in the court, and he was almost positive Henry would be no help. He'd probably give him a lecture about the importance of upholding laws.

He unlocked the first door, shuddering as it creaked open, then stepped quietly down the hall and waited, although he couldn't say what he waited for. His knock on the door split open the silence surrounding the prison walls, and he paused once more, waiting for a reaction—for better or worse.

Seconds went by, until those seconds became minutes. Duncan knocked again, three separate knocks, even and soft. Almost instantly, three similar knocks came back to him, as if mimicked.

"Are you in there?"

One knock sounded in the quiet, followed by another.

Duncan swallowed, a sudden nervousness infringing on the courage it had taken to come in the middle of the night. Dare he ask? "May I come in?"

A duo of knocks again penetrated the stillness of the dark hallway, the only light a mere sliver coming from underneath the door he'd closed behind him to prevent waking Thomas.

Trying to ward off the fear from gripping his heart, Duncan stuck the key into the lock and turned.

An intense darkness greeted him, and nothing else. He could not see her, nor anything, even his own fingers which he held directly in front of his eyes for a time. If she planned to kill him, it would most likely be easy in the darkness, and he would not fight back. He could never hurt her, although again, he could not say why. What was it about this girl that had called him back time and again?

"Are you sure you're in—"

"I'm over here."

Her voice had come from his left, where he guessed she sat in the corner. He remembered how she'd crouched or curled up in a ball in the far left corner of the outer prison cell.

Duncan knew solitary imprisonment came with no light, but he found himself wishing he'd brought a torch now.

"I've been hoping you'd come."

"Have you?" Duncan asked, surprised. Somehow he'd thought he'd be making all the conversation. "May I stay for a while?"

"Do I have a choice?" He could hear the despair in her voice, the fate she'd already accepted.

"As far as I'm concerned, yes. You will always have a choice with me."

Taking her silence as an affirmative, or if nothing else, a statement that she did not protest, Duncan closed the door slightly and took a few steps toward her in the darkness, using his hands to feel his way just in case some barrier stood between them.

Upon feeling a wall beneath his fingers, cold and coarse, he lowered his body and sat against it.

"Do you understand what is happening to you?"

"I am to be executed for murder. Hanged." She'd spoken it with almost no feeling, at least not that Duncan could hear. "Do you happen to know how long it is going to be?"

"Not exactly," Duncan answered. "Soon, I think. A few days, maybe."

"Oh."

"Are you frightened?"

"What is there to be afraid of? A cord around my neck? Losing my breath? Having nothing beneath my feet to catch and hold me in my moment of need? It seems to me dying can't be any worse than living. I have experienced all of those sensations before. The difference is I won't have to wake up and remember."

Duncan didn't know what to say, nor what to ask next. After learning about her past, he knew better than to ask her if she had any happy memories she would rather dwell on in her last hours. So he waited for her to speak again.

"Will you be there?" she asked. "When I die?"

This question forced Duncan to face what he'd been trying so desperately, yet so subtly, to avoid. A picture came to his mind, of her dangling from a rope tied to a wooden post, her hair wild again, because nobody had thought to brush it recently. "Why do you ask?" He shook the image from his head.

"I don't want you to be there. I don't want you to see me like that. If I have a choice with you, as you said a minute ago, I choose to have you somewhere else on the day I die."

All this talk of her death stirred something to life, a

thought at first, a simple idea. What if he could set her free? What if he could defy all the laws and even the condemnation of his brother and everyone in the castle? But to what end? Could she survive in this world? Would she go back to the barbarians, or would she live out the rest of her life alone?

"Do you have a name?" Duncan asked.

"The barbarians called me Shackle, because they said I came with shackles on my mind. I still don't know exactly what they meant."

"May I call you something else?"

"Like what?"

"Ovinia?"

She tried the name on her own lips, softly at first, then a little louder. "Hmmm," she said. "What does it mean?"

"I have no idea," Prince Duncan admitted.

Then a miracle happened. For the first time since he encountered her all those weeks ago, bloody and wild and being beaten out in the alley, she laughed. It rang and echoed in the darkness, sounding to Duncan much like the song of a contented bird: unassuming, pleasant, and gladly received. In that moment, Duncan discovered something within, a sense of purpose as he had never felt before. All those years he had spent escaping the castle early in the morning, avoiding his brother by skipping meals and refusing to go to council meetings, hiding the fact that he was a prince, seemed a waste now. All along he'd not really known why he hated it so badly, the prospect of being a prince, the destiny to rule. He knew now, listening to her laugh, what it felt like to have a purpose. Fearing she would stop, he began to laugh with her, a forced chuckle at first, then an uncontrollable laughter, heavy in his chest, tightening the muscles in his stomach, bringing a tear to his eye he was grateful she would never see.

"Why do you want to give me this name when you don't even know its meaning?" She asked through her lingering laughter.

Duncan shrugged. "I just heard it recently for the first time, and it made me think of you." For a brief moment, he thought of telling her she had a mother who cared about her very much, but a warning went of in his gut, gnawing and insuppressible. It would not be ignored, and Duncan knew better than to challenge it.

The laughter was gone now, just in time for them to hear a knock at the door. "Is someone in there?" It was Thomas.

A thick tension hung in the air now, and Duncan

worried she would try to attack him if he came in. "It's all right," he whispered. "I'll talk to him."

Duncan rose and walked blindly to the door, hands spread out before him. Thomas opened it a crack, which let in more light than Duncan expected. He must have had the entrance to the isolation hall propped open. "It's me, Prince Duncan."

"What on earth are you doing in there?" He asked it as if he thought Duncan crazy.

"I'm only speaking with her. She's calm, or was, until you came."

"You'll have to leave, your highness, or be locked in with her. I cannot leave this door open. I hope you'll understand."

"Of course I understand." He reached the keys out to him. "Let me know when the sun's been up an hour. I should go and help Henry with cleaning the castle."

"What happened to the castle?" Thomas asked.

"A fire. Nothing to worry about."

"I'm sorry Prince Duncan. Let me know if I can do anything to help."

"I will, Thomas. Thank you. You may leave us now."

The thought of his original purpose for coming out tonight brushed against Duncan's thoughts. He'd questioned the woman, discovered her guilt, and then let her go. He'd have to face Henry knowing the truth of that, but he could work that out later. He felt the keys being received and pulled from the grips of his palm. Then the light was gone again, and the lock clicked, the sound echoing softly.

"You're staying with me?"

"For a few hours at least."

Returning to his spot, or as close to it as he could get in the dark, Henry sat down again, instantly observing that he was nearer to her than he had been before, although he couldn't say exactly how he knew. Was her breathing a little louder? Or the essence of her skin a little closer? "Will you tell me what it was like living with the barbarians?"

"It's a way of life. Nothing more."

"Were you with them always? Are you one of them by birth?" Even though he knew the answer to these questions (as long as the witch had been telling the truth) he wanted to hear it from her own mouth, as much as she would tell.

"No." Duncan could hear something in her voice, some emotion. Disappointment? Shame? Fear?

"Where were you born then?"

"I don't know. I never had a father or mother, not that I can remember."

Thinking she would not want to tell him about her early life, if it was in fact true, Duncan began forming other questions, seeking to change the topic, but did not have the chance to speak any of them.

"I lived with others before the barbarians, two brothers, and one of them was married." It sounded as though she bowed her head now, the words coming softer, obstructed somehow by either the position of her head, or her unwillingness to share. "An awful woman."

"What were they like?"

"Barbarians with a roof over their head, cooked food, and no principles whatsoever. Even barbarians do not hurt the people they live with."

"These men, and this woman, did they hurt you?"

"Yes, badly."

"And so you left them?"

"Yes. Never to return. I was glad to be rid of them."

Duncan waited for it, but she never spoke of the murders. Perhaps she felt the regret of it now, the burden of having killed them, or the shame of not carrying it as a burden, the shame of feeling no remorse over something so severe.

"Tell me about *your* life," she said. Will you? Please?"

Duncan thought to select his words carefully at first, fearing to cause her further pain at the contrast between their situations, but decided being honest with her—completely honest—was the only way to continue building her trust.

"I had a marvelous childhood. Loving parents, a brother the exact same age to be my playmate, more food than I could ever eat, clean clothing, a castle."

"But something happened? Something bad?"

He marveled at her questions. Was he so easy to read? Could his despair be recognized in his voice, even as he spoke of such pleasant things? Or was she remembering their first encounter? When he'd shared that truth. "Yes, something bad happened."

"What was it?"

"My parents drowned at sea." She did not respond to this revelation, and Duncan hesitated, tortured by the silence, standing on the precipice of all those emotions he'd been denying and trying not to feel for so long, afraid to plunge into them, afraid she might push him over the edge.

Then a soft pressure fell on his left shoulder. Her fingertips. All this time, Duncan had been afraid to touch anything more than her hair, but he saw this as his chance, maybe his one and only chance, for a physical connection.

Reaching across his chest, he felt for her hand, and when he found it—cold, dry and stiff—he hugged it beneath his own, squeezing softly. The sound of her moving against the floor came next, followed by the touch of her side next to his, the pulling away of her hand, and in its place, her head resting against his arm. Surprised albeit delighted, Duncan wrapped one arm around her shoulders, and situated his opposite hand gently on her cheek.

Henry and the castle could wait. Duncan did not ever want to leave her side again.

15
Beauty

The sun burns bright, lighting up the scene before me, glinting through the glass of windows throughout the buildings along the corridors I can see from Henry's room. He's been asleep for hours, having nearly collapsed from exhaustion and been carried to his room by Duke and another servant whose name I never learned. The work continues on the main level, I imagine, and Duncan has never returned from going out to find her.

Henry stirs and I spin around, anxious to see him and have his full attention. It feels as though days have passed since we last spoke.

He murmurs something.

"Shhhhh," I say.

"What time is it?"

"It doesn't matter. Not today. Just rest." I stand beside his bed, caught up in the image of him. He turns onto his back and looks up at me, resting one arm underneath his head, staring into my eyes, lost in some thought he keeps to himself. Still in the soot covered shirt from the night before, he looks older, though his wild hair and the dirt all over his pillowcase remind me of a boy who tires himself playing outside, only to crash into bed before having a bath.

"What are you thinking about?" I ask, not able to bare the silent stare any longer. It makes me nervous, the way he studies me.

He does not answer right away, as if he is daydreaming or he didn't quite hear me.

"Nothing," he says. "Any sign of Duncan?"

"Not that I've heard or seen."

Reaching for the bell, he cries out in pain.

"I'll get that," I say, but I stop before I realize that I can't get it. All my fears and apprehension return in an instant and it angers me, how helpless I feel. How helpless I am.

"Don't fret, Eglantine. It's only a sore muscle." Holding onto a shoulder with one hand, he reaches for the bell again.

"Eglantine, I am going to have Duke come and prepare a bath. Will you please excuse me for an hour or so?"

"Of course."

"See if you can find out anything about Duncan, or the woman who started the fire."

Feeling a little like a servant, I hesitate, resenting his words the way I always resented my parents telling me what to do as a child.

"Will you? Please?" His soft, genuine plea calls me back from the willfulness that had been brewing inside. "For me?"

Softening his command into a polite request stills my resentment. Happy to do as he asks, I nod at him, smiling at the way his hair sticks out all round his head, like a porcupine after getting entangled in a briar bush.

"Oh, and Eglantine?"

Having nearly reached the door, I turn back to him.

"When I am cleaned and dressed, there is something I would like to talk to you about. Will you please meet me in the garden?"

Duke enters the room, and rather than keep Henry's attention anymore, I nod at him and abandon the vicinity.

Since I cannot ask anyone about Duncan, I stop near every group of servants or men still working in the kitchen and listen. A giant hole reveals the outside from the kitchen wall, and all the wooden fixtures in the room have burned, but the damage has been localized, thankfully. For the most part, they work in silence, I guess feeling the weight of such an occurrence and the laborious aftermath.

After a time, I decide Henry and I are the only ones aware of Duncan's absence. It was not unusual after all, for him to be away from the castle for so long.

I wait in the garden until Henry returns, imagining I can smell the roses, but with every sniff a whisper of mint spreads through me instead. Rounding a hedge and looking toward the castle, I see Henry standing there, his arms behind his back, tucked in and dressed as formal as he had been the night before, hair sitting in its normal downward position. How long has he been watching me? I smile at him, but it is a cautious smile. What is it he wants to talk to me about? Perhaps he's had the chance to think about my suggestion that I go home. Perhaps he finally agrees with me. But as much as I had meant what I said in the moment, I did not want to leave him, and the thought of doing so causes a squeezing pressure in my heart. I can scarcely breath.

"Hello," he says, his lips in a straight line as they are most often.

I smile, feeling foolish as I had the night before, standing before him in my white nightgown with rumpled hair while he's dressed like a king.

"Will you sit with me?"

I nod and we both move toward the bench from opposite sides until we are sitting next to one another.

"Eglantine, I want to tell you something."

Still fearful he will ask me to leave, I feel the sweat forming on my forehead and under my arms. It is real, which causes more discomfort because I am worried he will notice.

"I know that in reality you are sleeping, and that you are far away. But I also know that I have never been happier than I am with you here. I know that I never want you to leave."

Stunned and flattered, I allow my spirit to rise a little, his words bringing a glowing confidence to my chest. But it is in vain, and the thought of my state crushes it back down, my pointless, helpless state.

"Eglantine, there is something more I need to say. Something I wish to ask. If it is all right with you?"

I nod, wanting sincerely to know what it is he would like to ask me.

"If you were not sleeping, and you and I had met over the years in other circumstances, do you think we would be as good of friends as we are now?"

"I suppose so."

"And if the curse was broken—let's say today or tomorrow—would you be open to me . . ." He looks down, his hands resting on the bench as his body faces me.

"What?" I ask, frustrated that he paused in the middle of his sentence. What was he struggling so much to ask me?

His eyes find mine again, and with a deep breath, he finally finds the words. "Would you marry me? Under either of those circumstances, do you think you would agree to marry me?"

I think about it for a moment, feeling secure in the imaginary. "Nothing would make me as happy."

I begin examining my answer, searching my heart, wondering if it is the prospect of being free that is so enticing, or the idea of being married to Henry. A breeze sweeps through the garden, billowing the arms of his shirt and displacing the hair across his forehead. I can hear it, and see the effects, but no air moves with such force over my skin. I am immune to it. In that moment, I discover my own heart, what it would mean to be free, what it would mean to be with Henry permanently and actually, and what it would mean to have them both together.

"*Nothing* would make me as happy."

The intensity of his gaze after that sends a spark through my chest, an electric pulse that shocks my very soul, and then it settles into a warm sensation around my heart, constant and comforting, and I know by the expectant look on his face he isn't finished with his question.

"Eglantine, if you would be happy to marry me under those circumstances, I wonder . . . would you be willing to take my hand as we are? To marry me as we both are now?"

The door of the castle opens behind us, and Duke walks out onto the lawn. I wonder why he did not just step out of the hole in the wall.

Henry looks at me rather than him, waiting for my answer.

"We've had word of Master Duncan," Duke says.

But Henry ignores him, still eager to receive my reply.

A hot tear seeps from my eye and onto my cheek. I nod.

Henry breathes out a sigh of relief, bowing his head toward me and taking a few more deep breaths before turning to Duke.

"Where is he?"

"He's in prison, sire."

"In prison? What happened?"

"He stays with *her*, your majesty. The girl in prison sentenced to die."

"Find him. Tell him I need to see him. It's urgent."

Duke leaves us and Henry looks into my lap where my hands are resting.

"I would give anything to hold you in my arms right now."

The tears continue, some of them joyful, and some of them full of sorrow, knowing he will never be able to hold me as he wishes.

He reaches for my hands. "Don't cry, Eglantine. I will never regret my choice, no matter what happens. If you stay cursed forever, I will be happy always to have you near my side. I don't ever want to lose you."

Standing up, he asks me to follow him. We enter the castle again and the first person he locates is Marie. Leaning in close to her ear, he whispers, "Marie, will you please prepare the ballroom? I would like it adorned with an array of flower arrangements, and please set out some refreshments."

"Yes, your majesty. When would you like it to be ready?"

"As soon as possible. Please let me know once it is

finished."

She nods and turns to leave.

"Oh, Marie," Henry calls after her. "Will you also send for a magistrate?"

I can tell it is a strange request by the look in her eye, the confusion furrowing her brow.

"Please, Marie."

"Very well, your majesty."

We walk back out to the garden, I think because Henry needs the fresh air.

"Are you worried?" I ask him.

"Worried? About what?"

"About what they will think of you."

Our arms reach out a little, as if we are holding hands. He shakes his head. "No, Eglantine. I'm not. Are you?"

"I'm not worried for my sake." I stop floating along side him and wait for him to face me. "I only worry for you. Will they think you're mad, or lose their respect for you?"

"Eglantine, stop. We are getting married. I need you to be strong now. Forget about what they think. It will only be Duke and Duncan anyway, besides the magistrate. I don't want you to concern yourself with their opinions of me."

I nod, but the discovery—or perhaps the realization of what I could not admit on my own—that I am to be his secret wife, as if he is ashamed of me, cuts deep. I know it is the best way, perhaps even the only way, but it still stings a little, still leaves me feeling . . . alone.

Circling around the garden time and time again, we see servants come out and cut flowers. We even see Duncan return to the castle although he does not see us, not even Henry. And we see the magistrate's carriage arriving by the front gate.

"Are you ready for this?" he asks.

I nod, my head high, my mind sure.

After entering the castle through the back door once more, Duncan is the first we see. Duke is close by him.

"What is it?" Duncan asks. "What has happened?"

"Nothing, yet. But I wanted you to be here when it does. Duke, will you please join the three of us in the ballroom?"

Duke looks around for another, but does not question his master. As we walk through the entrance hall, Henry spots the magistrate and after thanking him for coming on such short notice, beckons him to follow also.

The ballroom is bright, the rays of sunshine coming through the tall windows and making irregular rectangle shapes of light across the floor. I imagine the fragrance of the freshly cut flowers: roses and jasmine.

"What's going on, Henry?" Duncan asks.

Without a hint of a second thought, Henry answers. "I'm getting married."

"Well, congratulations, Master Henry." Duke stretches out his hand to him and they shake. "Who is the lucky lady?"

"It is Eglantine. From Cray. She is here with me now and we would like to be married right away. This very minute."

"Have you gone mad?" Duncan's harsh tone slices through the air as the hopeful joy of a few moments before flees away. Or perhaps there had been more trepidation than I could confess even to myself. I feel it now, all the nerves and hesitation, wondering whether we are making the right choice.

But Henry does not falter, and I feel unworthy of his constancy for all my vacillation.

"No, Duncan." He is as cool and calm as still ocean water. "I know I am not mad. You have seen her for yourself. We wish to be married. It's done. Or will be shortly."

"Master Duncan has seen her?" Duke asks.

Turning a little pink, perhaps afraid to be seen as a lunatic like his brother, Duncan shifts his eyes between the three other men in the room. "Well, yes, I've seen her, but . . ."

"That settles it. Magistrate, will you please take your place. You may stand over there, near the fire." The most complacent, he obeys Henry with no argument.

"Good. And I'll stand on one side, and then . . . here, Eglantine." He gestures for me to stand across from him in front of the magistrate.

"And the two of you may stand wherever you'd like."

Duncan and Duke exchange a look. I watch them, wondering if they will try to intervene, or come up with a plan to postpone the wedding and call for a doctor. After a moment, they both shrug and move a little closer to us.

I smile, grateful they do not see any harm in it, or if they do, they are keeping it to themselves. Henry whispers to the magistrate my full name: Eglantine Cordelia Argall, princess of Cray.

I watch Henry as they exchange a few words I do not hear, focusing on first his brow, and then his jaw, an overwhelming gratitude filling my soul that he is choosing me; that he even noticed me in the first place; that he asked me to stay with him; that he is vowing now to never send me away.

The voice of the magistrate is quiet, as if he is afraid others will learn what he is doing. But other than this, there is no sign or hint of his disapproval. Dressed in a white shirt and black breeches with a black doublet and dark leather shoes, he looks dressed for court. I had seen a few of them in previous weeks, occasionally walking about the castle and attending a council meeting when invited.

He proceeds to utter the ceremony, but I concentrate so completely on Henry that I do not hear every word. When he pauses, I realize he has been speaking to me and is waiting for an answer. "Yes," I say.

"How will we know if she's said yes?" Duncan asks, a residual irritation creeping out with the tone of his voice. They hurt, those words he speaks, his continually questioning my existence even though I sang him to sleep all those days ago.

"Pay him no mind," Henry whispers, staring straight at me, not giving any attention to Duncan's question. "She has answered yes, magistrate."

Then the man speaks to Henry, and I hear the words this time, asking Henry if he will accept me, cherish me all my days, and keep me well and safe to the best of his ability. A resounding, "Yes," echoes through the room, and it chills me with excitement that he would proclaim such love and loyalty, that he is marrying me as I am, a mirage of sorts in his world.

"Then by the power bestowed upon me by the former king of Fallund, I introduce you as husband and wife, bound together for your existence here in this mortal world."

I think of the word 'existence,' let it sink deep into my mind. Maybe the magistrate can't see me, or Duke, or Duncan at this very moment, but I do in fact exist. Henry steps toward me, as close as he can get without going right through me, and bends down, his eyes closed. I press my lips to his, or try anyway, and it is over. Done. Finished. Henry and I are married.

"I'm sorry there is no music," he whispers in my ear. "Or I would ask you to dance."

"I remember well what happened last time, and I can honestly say I'm glad we're not going to try that again." I smile at him, giddy and carefree until Duncan invades our space.

"You're insane. You know that, right?"

Henry turns to his brother. "I'm not insane. Just in love. Tell me, Brother, why do you keep going back to that prison?"

Duncan searches Henry's eyes. I watch him for a time, standing there, not willing to answer the question.

"Is it because you have found something that makes you happy? Something that gives you a sense of purpose?" Not waiting for a response, Henry continues. "Well, that is all I have done. And rather than stand by helpless, I have taken matters into my own hands. Isn't that what we have to do sometimes? Take matters into our own hands?" They share a look, a secret look, as if communicating through only a stare, and I am left on the outside, never to understand what they are saying to one another. Somehow I don't mind. Duncan can go sit on a pin for all I care. A big, sharp one.

Duke approaches next. "I think I am supposed to congratulate you, sire. Although, I'm not exactly sure what is happening here."

"Don't fret, Duke. All is well." They shake hands again. Henry invites the men to help themselves to the small table of refreshments, but he does not partake. I think it is most likely because he knows I cannot eat it, and he does not want me to feel left out.

Duncan leaves first, after asking Henry to congratulate me for him. I do not find I am less agitated with him even for the kind gesture, no matter how sincere.

"I love you," Henry whispers to me as the magistrate and Duke are leaving. The door closes behind them, and a trace of lavender fills my senses, even though there isn't any in the room.

16

BEAST

Dawn crept in slowly, and its appearance would be subtle because of the cloud cover. Even the inside air felt damp. Duncan had been awake for a time, dressing first in his old peasant disguise—thankfully it'd been laundered since he'd worn it last—and packing a small bag with a few changes of clothes and personal items, including a small painting of Henry and himself from when they were children, the only memorabilia he'd be taking from the castle.

After grabbing the letter for Henry he'd penned the night before from off his writing desk, he made his way to Henry's room. Still baffled by the wedding scene of the day before, he mused for a moment over the possible ramifications of what he was about to do. Had Henry actually lost his mind? Or was he in the process? How would the kingdom fare? If Eglantine remained cursed forever, as the witch had said she would, where would that leave Henry?

None of it was his concern anymore, though the

prospect of his brother in trouble (including troubles of the heart) still caused him to worry, especially while he remained in the castle, the memories of the past and the uncertainty of the future all intermingling and straining the fibers of his brain. Those worries would lessen over time, he hoped.

Duncan opened the door a fraction to see if Henry slept or if he'd already awoken. Only a smidgen of light came through the window, filtered by a thin white curtain, only a hint of the coming day, dampened by the darkness of the stormy sky. Henry slept. Quite alone, Duncan noted, wondering if Eglantine was somehow nearby and how often she came to him in the visions of her dreams.

Determined, Duncan marched to his bedside and shook his shoulder.

"Henry, wake up."

After mumbling for a moment, Henry shot up. "What is it?"

"Shhhhh. Calm down." Duncan had rehearsed this interaction several times already, but somehow, looking down at his brother, his heart grew heavy, a little unwilling to go through with his plan. "How are you?"

Henry looked up at his brother. "Is that really why you woke me up? To ask me how I am?" He sounded in a bad mood, but waking him early was the only way.

"I'm leaving."

Henry rubbed his eyes now. "Is that all? You've never felt it necessary to let me know before. What makes today different?"

Ignoring the sarcasm, Duncan continued, resolved to be straightforward. "I'm not coming back."

Throwing his covers off, Henry swung his legs around so they dangled over the edge of his bed. Bracing himself by gripping the mattress with his hands on both sides, Henry opened his eyes, fully aware now, staring at his brother. "What do you mean?"

"I thought about what you said yesterday. I'm taking matters into my own hands." Duncan held out the letter. "My renunciation."

Henry took the letter, ran his fingers over the seal, and then ripped it open, pulling out the folded parchment and opening it. He read slowly, and when he was finished, let out a deep sigh. "You're leaving with her?"

"Yes, Henry. I thought you might not understand, but I want you do know what I have learned. I heard her story once, what others knew of her and how she was abused and beaten. The man she was accused of murdering was her abuser. She did it out of fear. Fear of being imprisoned again. She did it to defend herself. She too has confirmed these stories down to every detail. I believe her, I love her."

Henry began folding the letter back up and stuffing it in the envelop once more. "I will make sure they do not hunt you down."

Duncan smiled at that. Despite his faults, Henry was loyal to the core. "Thank you, Brother."

"Will I ever see you again?"

"I hope."

"How will I get a hold of you?"

"Not by sending Worston." Duncan smiled bigger now, and Henry smiled back. "I plan to take her north, into Cray or close to the seashore of Fallund. There is a little village near there. Gilmuck."

"Will you write?"

"I'll try." He smiled deviously. He'd never been good at sending correspondence.

Henry stood now, facing his brother.

"Can I offer you some advice?" Duncan asked.

"Advice? I've been trying to get you to give me some advice for years now. It's been like pulling walrus teeth, and now you're giving it for free?"

"I always was full of surprises."

"That you were. Tell me. What is your advice?"

"Let Duke take my place. Not as your brother. But as your closest adviser. He is wise, and loyal."

"But Duke's a servant."

"Yes. A wise and loyal servant. You can find another butler. Have Karl for all I care, though he's not as bright."

Duncan could see Henry was contemplating the idea, and the weight of this goodbye pressed even more firmly upon him. "Goodbye, Brother." Not sure whether Henry would find an embrace awkward, he hesitated, trying to decide whether to lift a hand for a shake, or to raise both arms for a hug. But he didn't have to decide, for Henry grabbed him by the shoulder blades and pulled him into a crushing squeeze. Duncan hugged him back, then felt repeated slaps on his back as well.

"I'll miss you too."

Choking back the emotion, Duncan slipped away from his brother and toward the door.

"Duncan," Henry called. "If you should ever need anything, don't hesitate to ask."

Duncan nodded. "Thank you, Brother. It means a lot."

"What happened to the woman? The witch who started the fire?"

"I couldn't find her."

Regretting only slightly that his last words to his brother were a lie, Duncan walked out of the room, down the tower steps, and out the front castle door.

Still quiet from the lingering night, the corridors and alleys reminded Duncan of what castle life had been since the death of his parents, sparse and lonely. He thought of them, their mother greeting Henry and him in the morning when they were young and sipping tea with them in later years; their father taking a moment or two to play or talk in between his meetings; the family dinners at the royal dining table every single night. So much had changed, and just like there was no going back to the way things had been before, there was no going back on his decision. Duncan abandoned the sentiments as a nagging nervousness seeped into his gut. He could wallow in nostalgia later; now he needed to focus on getting her out unscathed.

Slipping a healthy length of rope from underneath his shirt, Henry reached the prison and peeked inside. He had brought it in case the man guarding needed some coercion to let them go.

Phillip lay sleeping on the guard bed down the steps from the prison doorway. Without a second thought, Duncan moved forward, having brought the spare keys from the castle. Without hesitation, he opened the first door, strode through the hall, and unlocked the final barrier between them.

She stood facing the far wall. Not even the light coming through the door seemed to stir her attention.

"Ovinia?" he whispered.

Hearing his voice, she turned to face him.

"I've come to free you, to help you escape. I make no promises except this one: if we make it out alive, I will stay by your side never to leave you again."

A trace of doubt flickered in her eyes, her expression otherwise unreadable, and then a huge smile formed on her lips and she ran to him, jumping into his arms and holding on tight to his neck.

Duncan held onto her waist, basking in the embrace for a moment. "We need to get moving."

"One thing," she said as she turned from him and retrieved her silver brush from the grainy floor.

Duncan took note of his pounding heart. Gripping the rope tightly, he thought if they just hurried, they could quietly escape without even being noticed.

"Is someone there?" called a voice.

Ovinia hurried to the prince's side and grasped his arm. Duncan whispered a reassurance. "Hold on to me and everything will be all right."

Duncan loosened the rope slightly, preparing to use it as soon as they made their presence known. He knew fear was on their side, as the guards were all still sore afraid of her, but he was ready to fight if necessary. Pulling on her hand, Duncan led her slowly back down the hallway.

Unexpectedly, a single loud, quick thud sounded, followed shortly by a body slumping to the floor. Pausing for a moment, listening only to the sounds of their breathing, Duncan wrapped one arm around Ovinia's shoulders. Carefully, Duncan guided her out to the main portion of the prison. Phillip lay on the floor, a trickle of blood coming from his forehead.

"What happened?" Ovinia asked. Duncan could hear the panic in her voice.

"I'm not sure." Walking her to the door, Duncan took a moment to scan the alley before they made their way outside the prison walls. "Let's run for it."

A spark of fearful energy ran through Duncan. Clasping hands, they ran away from the castle, away from the prison, away from the rows and down Northeast Alley, at the end of which he hoped would be the carriage he'd asked Karl to bring. Behind them Duncan could hear the faint chatter of merchants coming out to open their shops;

he should have come a little earlier. "Don't look back," he said, as much to himself as to Ovinia.

Reaching the end of the alley, they rounded the final corner, the first glimpse of the vast countryside emerging. The carriage was there, as was . . . "Worston?" Breathless, Duncan halted, pulling Ovinia to a stop as well as his boots skidded across the dirt. "What on earth are you doing here?"

The man's wicked smile set off an alarm in Duncan. He'd avoided killing so far today—or even tying anyone up—and hoped he could keep with that tradition, but something in this man provoked him like nothing else, a thorn from childhood that would not be removed.

"Karl asked me to bring the carriage. Said you'd be taking an early morning ride."

Karl could be such an idiot. He'd probably thought having Worston come would not only save him the trouble, but provide a way for the prince's watch guard to easily find him.

"You are a hard man to follow, Prince Duncan. And who is this?" He began circling Ovinia. "Too plain to have a rendezvous with a member of the royal family, surely. This isn't her, is it? The convicted murderer everyone's been talking about? The one you have some freakish obsession with?"

Duncan glanced at Ovinia, trying to determine if his words were igniting something dangerous in her. She looked calm, but taking care of the problem sooner rather than later would be a good preemptive measure. Thinking for a moment of the few men he'd killed in battle, before he had been pierced himself and fell out of the fight, Duncan tried to catch hold of the bravery he'd needed then. Besides, he'd hit Worston before. It had been a pleasure.

Worston interrupted his thoughts. "You know, I have no interest in the girl, and don't really care what you do with her. But you'll have to buy my silence." The smirk on his face angered Duncan even more. He carried money, but they needed it to survive on, and he would not give even a tiny portion to the imbecile standing before him.

Preparing his fist for the blow, Duncan pulled his arm away from Ovinia, giving her a little shove to the side. Before he could take a swing, a dark figure moved from somewhere behind the carriage.

It was the woman, Ovinia's mother, the witch who'd cursed Eglantine and started the castle fire. She held something in her hand, but Duncan couldn't tell what. With her speedy approach, Worston rambled fearfully about his right to earn a living, about the injustice of escaped prisoners, about witches . . . and then, THWACK. The black and gray haired woman had smacked him in the head with what looked like a heavy stone. His eyes rolled back and he slumped over, falling to the ground with a single thump.

"Thank you," Duncan said. And then he didn't know what to say. There they all stood, on the brink of something: a word, a question, Duncan didn't quite know what. Did she want an invitation to come with them?

Thinking he should at least introduce them, Duncan gently caught hold of Ovinia's arm once more. "Ovinia, this is . . . well, I don't know her name. But don't be frightened."

"Magnolia." She held out her hand, taking a slow, cautious step forward. "My name is Magnolia. I have often been called Maggie."

Ovinia looked at Duncan, as if seeking his approval, or perhaps just looking for some reassurance that it was safe.

Duncan nodded at her, pulling her even closer to him for comfort.

"I'm Ovinia."

"Yes, I know, child." The woman smiled broadly, showing her overlapping teeth and the places where no teeth could be found, even though they should have been there.

"Your journey will be long?" she asked.

"Not too long," Duncan answered as he felt Ovinia take hold of his arm again.

The witch looked to her daughter then, as if trying to decide if she had grabbed hold of him out of fear.

"Are you going somewhere yourself?" Duncan asked.

"I don't know what I'll do next."

Leaning forward, Duncan whispered to her. "We're traveling north. To the seashore. Would you like a ride? We'll be traveling by carriage for a time, but then we will abandon it and walk. You could have the horse. We'd never be able to keep it."

She looked at the horse.

"Or you could come with us," he offered.

Ovinia's grip tightened on his arm, and the witch seemed to notice.

"Oh, I couldn't trouble you." Waving her hand, she dismissed the idea, then looked sternly at Duncan. "Take care of her."

"I will."

After taking one last glance at her daughter, the woman turned to leave.

Duncan helped Ovinia into the carriage, assuring her that he would be right back. Catching up with the woman, he stopped her. "Are you sure you won't come with us?"

She paused, looked at the used-to-be prince, and gave her answer. "It is enough that I know she is free. I could ask for nothing more. She trusts *you,* but that is where it ends. It would not be good for her if I came, nor do I believe it would benefit her to know who I am." Nodding as she took a deep breath, she thought for a moment. "It is better for her to move on. Maybe better for me as well. But I thank you. I can rest now."

Could she, truly? "What about Eglantine?" Duncan asked, thinking once more of his poor brother, and the sleeping princess whom he loved.

She stared at him intently for a moment. "I don't know why you are so interested in her, but unless there are some other powers at work, I'm afraid her condition is permanent." After speaking, Magnolia turned to walk away.

A sinking feeling entered his chest, probably because while Henry had given him the courage and reassurance to follow his heart, he could do nothing for him in return. Coming back to the carriage, Duncan looked up to see Ovinia's worried face.

"Was I gone too long?"

The sun inched up from the horizon. Duncan

watched it through the carriage window, just to the side of her face. She turned to see it as well, and then reached her hand out to him, inviting him to join her.

17

Beauty

Ocean waves roar in my ear, louder and clearer than ever before. The strong scent of mint bites at my nose, causing me to stir in my bed. And I hear a bird, chirping incessantly, as if warning an enemy to stay away from its nest. The sun is hot on my skin, piercing through the glass, and bright even through my closed eyelids.

I blink once, opening my eyes for a split second and closing them again. The light is blinding, painful, and I keep them closed.

Where am I?

I search my memory. I had been watching Henry sleep, standing at the window, anticipating the sunrise because it meant he would wake and I could see him again. Duncan had come in. They'd spoken, bid farewell, and then Duncan left. He wasn't coming back. I allow this to sink in, knowing how hurt Henry must be. We'd been walking in the garden not long after that, and Henry began to grow dim. At first, I thought it because the weather.

Clouds covered every inch of sky, and a layer of thick fog floated around us.

I open my eyes again, and blink several times. The plants are clustered around me, their colors so vibrant—green leaves, purple lavender, white lilies with orange spots in the center.

What has happened?

I lean up on my elbow, looking around. Am I in another dream? I have never seen such color in any of my dreams. Thinking of the roses outside, which I can barely glimpse through the vines crawling up the glass, I wonder if I am to run outside, find the dead ones, and water them with my tears.

Then something moves outside the glass, walking toward me, rustling through the shrubs.

I look to the door, unprepared for whatever surprise lurks in this dream. Will it be the witch? Coming to my resting place rather than the woods? A figure enters through the door and the relief floods through me. It is Stella. What will happen next?

She walks around for a while, unaware of me. A bunch of leafy stems are pulled from her bag, and she prepares the surface of a small table, brushing it clean with her free hand. Then she grasps a knife and begins to chop the leaves.

"Stella?"

She turns toward me. "Eglantine!" Dropping the knife and bunch of stems, she runs to me. "Eglantine, you're awake!"

"Stella, what has happened?"

Her arms fly around me and I fall backward, the weight of her crushing me as she refuses to let go.

"Stella, please get off." As she pulls back, I study her face, clear and bright as the morning sun on a cloudless sky, the outline of her body firm against the background, not blurred as in my dreams. Sitting up, I gaze into her pearly blue eyes, and her huge smile forces a smile from me too. She sits beside me and I throw my arms around her.

"I'm awake." As my head rests against her shoulder, I peer through the glass, straining to see through all the creeping vines, and there it is, the thunderous ocean, waves rushing and clapping. A deep happiness swells inside me, and for a moment I feel whole, complete.

Then I think of Henry, and if it wasn't for the sight of the ocean, I imagine my heart would break. "It's raining in Fallund."

Pushing me away, Stella asks, "What are you talking about?"

With her hands still clamped to my arms, I answer. "It is raining in Fallund." I look up for a moment, wondering how the sun dare to shine so bright here in Cray when the skies are dark and misty in Henry's kingdom. "I have to go to Fallund."

Pushing Stella away, I try to move my legs, but while my mind is alert and active, my body is trembling, my legs unwilling, perhaps even unable.

"No, you must rest. I will have the guards send for your parents."

I dread the thought of lying back down, but my body is so weak that if it doesn't happen voluntarily, and soon, I will surely collapse.

Stella leaves and I am left alone once again, panic seeping into my mind and heart, reaching out and touching every part of me. I worry for Henry and what he must be thinking now that I'm gone. Had I floated away from him, or simply vanished? What had he done then? Was he still in the garden, calling my name and searching for the vision of me?

"Two of the guards are sailing back to the castle."

I look in her direction and am surprised to see such a large group of men surrounding her, each dressed for battle, each armed with a sword. It brings me comfort, to know Father and Mother went to such lengths to protect me, even though they'd sent me away from the castle.

"Good day, your highness," one of them says, smiling like an idiot. They are all smiling, all apparently in awe to see me.

"All right, you've seen her. Now return to your posts. Prepare to receive the king and queen." She tries to wave them away with her arms, but they linger and gawk, moving slowly to follow her directions.

It is agony waiting for Father and Mother. Will Aunt Cornelia be with them? I will be so glad to see them all, but the thought of Henry gnaws at me. I close my eyes, trying with all my might to settle my brain, to find the rest that will lead me to my dreams again. I want to find Henry.

It is no use. The spell is broken, and having slept for most of my life, I am not remotely tired.

I watch the ship getting closer, able only to see it in patches because of all the greenery, but it grows bigger and bigger to my view as it approaches. A giddy excitement dances in my stomach, like a million tiny moths flapping their wings inside me.

"They're here," Stella says, standing to leave.

I hear voices calling in the distance, some the low voices of men, others the alto voices of women. Then they are running toward me, the sound of their quick paces thrashing *through* shrubbery rather than around it. I only catch a glimpse of their movements through the glass, but in a moment they are at the door, looks of wonderment on their faces: Father, Mother, Aunt Cornelia, all come to see the miracle of my wakefulness.

Mother clasps a hand over her mouth as she lets out a joyful gasp. Her other hand moves to her stomach. Father's face sends a rush of nostalgia, like breathing a pleasantly familiar scent. He looks as he ever did: trimmed beard and moustache, dark eyes, thin face. Other than the fact he hunches over more than he used to, and the few deep wrinkles on his skin, he looks the same. They rush to me, along with Aunt Cornelia and her bright smile, her hair a lively reddish-brown.

Mother reaches me first. Her arms slide underneath my back and she pulls me to her. I wrap my arms around her head, feeling her soft curls beneath my fingers. Father wraps his arms around us, and Aunt Cornelia leans in, wrapping an arm around my shoulder. I lean my head into her and soak it all up, basking in the comfort of their attention and embraces.

"Can she walk?" Father asks Stella.

"She hasn't tried yet, but I don't think she is strong

enough. It will take time."

"I'll carry her." Father lifts me up and walks me to the ship. I hate that I cannot set my bare feet in the glistening sand. So long I've waited to see the shore, to run along the beach, and now that I am awake, I am too weak. A part of me—just a sliver, or perhaps more—prefers dreaming, where I am able to move as I please most of the time, where I can even fly.

The voyage is short, less than an hour it seems; the sun has barely moved in the sky from what I can tell.

A small welcoming party is there to greet us, mostly servants. A face or two is familiar. All are smiling, and a few of them have tear stained cheeks.

"Welcome home, Princess Eglantine," someone says. I don't see who. I am anxious to get in the castle, anxious to tell my parents what has happened.

Inside, a table is set for tea. The five of us sit down—Father, Mother, Aunt Cornelia, Stella and I—Father putting me in a chair and propping me up with a few pillows.

What are they going to think? What are they going to say when they begin talking? I decide to begin the conversation.

"Father, Mother." It is good to address them, to hear their names in my own voice and feel the words spoken on my tongue and lips. "There is something I need to tell you."

"What is it, darling?" Mother asks before pressing the white porcelain teacup to her mouth.

"I need to go to Fallund. As soon as possible."

Father chuckles. "Impossible."

I watch him leaning back in his chair, mouth curved up in a proud smile, one hand gripping the handle of the teacup as it rests on the table.

"Then I need you to write the king. Tell him I am all right. Tell him I am awake and that I want him to come to Cray. To meet my parents." I look at my aunt. "To meet all of you."

"What are you talking about, my little dumpling?" It has never bothered me before, maybe it couldn't in my sleep, but that name rubs against my nerves like a ship screeching against a rock hidden beneath the water.

"I'm talking about the fact that I am married to the king of Fallund."

Father's face changes in an instant, the smile gone, replaced with the most serious look I've ever seen on him. He looks to Stella for an explanation. "Stella, what is this nonsense?"

"I don't know, your majesty."

"Perhaps she is tired from the journey and the

excitement of it all," Mother says.

"I am not tired."

Father stands and swoops me up again. "I'm taking her to her room. Stella, please bring some tonic."

How can he think of forcing me to sleep after I've been gone for so many years? It is as if they do not know what to do with me, now that I am awake and have a voice. Or perhaps they think I'm mad, talking of the king of Fallund.

"It's true, Father. And I need to write to him."

Ignoring me, he heads for the door and up the small staircase that leads to the hallway where a set of tower stairs are. Soon I am sitting up in my bed, staring out my old window, the sea waving to me from below.

"If you will not write him, I will." Mother and Aunt Cornelia have stayed downstairs. I'm sure Stella will be here shortly, but it is only Father and I now.

As he paces across my floor, he watches me, and I am forced to see it, the concern written on his face.

Stella comes in, holding a tray with a bottle of tonic. I can taste it in my mouth before she even gets close, remembering all those times I'd been given it against my will, all those times I'd met the witch in the forest. As she pours a spoonful I seal my lips shut, and when she holds the spoon out to me, I whack it away with my arm.

"Eglantine, stop!" Father commands. "Stop this nonsense and take it." He turns to Stella. "What is happening? Is it the curse?"

"I don't know, your majesty."

"Try again."

Then I realize that taking the tonic may force me to sleep where before it had been impossible. I could see Henry. I keep my lips sealed, pretending that I do not want it, and hold my chin up high.

"There, there, Eglantine. You don't want it spilling all over your bed, do you?"

I turn away from the spoon, but when she squeezes at my cheeks and shoves it in my mouth, I allow the bitter liquid to slide onto my tongue and down my throat. I swallow hard, glaring at them both, and then lie down, shifting my arms and my pillows until I am comfortable.

Father pulls my sheet and blanket up to my neck. "Rest well, my love."

"Goodnight, Father." I never could stay angry at him for long.

Sleep enfolds me, so much so that I feel the blankets have me tied up. I open my eyes to darkness. I am in the woods. As I rise up from the floor, the blanket wrapped around me falls to the ground silently. Floating in the air, I turn this way and that, contemplating which way to go, hoping I choose the right direction, the one that leads me away from her.

Spreading out my arms to fly, I move up above the trees, hovering over the landscape. The ocean is in the distance, and there, resting near the shore is my little house of glass, covered in vines that are all dried up, lifeless and brittle. It takes a moment to get moving, but I will myself toward it, longing to get away from the forest.

When I reach it, I hover over it for a moment, and then sink down through the roof. Henry enters then, frantic and calling my name as one arm rests against the door.

"Henry?" I call.

He looks all around. I don't think he heard me.

"Henry!"

"Eglantine? Is that you?"

"Henry, I'm up here."

"Eglantine, I can barely hear you. Where are you?"

"I'm in the castle. Sleeping." The words fall out of my mouth, losing their power it seems as soon as they reach the air.

"I will find you," he says. "I will find you."

The picture of him standing there at the door, the

glass walls all around me, the dying plants, it all begins to fuzz out and fade away until I see only blackness.

* * *

The sound of a voice first catches my attention. I try to focus on it, try to figure out who is speaking. It is Stella, I think. No, Mother. She reads to me, a story that is almost familiar, and I wonder if I know it from my childhood, or perhaps she used to read it to me on her visits. Her voice grows more powerful as I wake more and more until it is clear as a cloudless sky. I keep my eyes closed for a time and just listen.

It has been days since I first woke up.

Days of fighting them.

Pleading.

It always ends in the tonic and trying to find Henry in a dream.

He is lost to me; I have not been able to locate him since that first day I dreamed he came to find me in the glasshouse.

"Her breathing has changed." That is Stella. She never misses a thing. "She may be waking up."

"Eglantine, are you awake?" It is Aunt Cornelia, and I feel the pressure of her sitting beside me, followed by a warm hand covering my own. I open my eyes to see her face. Mother is close by also, leaning in, her eyes the color of the dark blue ocean. I smile at them, but do not speak, afraid they do not want to hear what I have to say.

"Can I get you anything?" Stella asks. "Something to eat, or a drink of water?"

Something to eat. I used to think all I wanted was to take a bite of a salty chunk of ham, or feel the duo of bread and butter on my tongue. I shake my head.

"Stella, bring Bartholomew. He asked to be notified as soon as she woke."

I do not want to see my father, not now.

Stella leaves me with Mother and Aunt Cornelia. I enjoy their admiring stares, feeling loved and wanted, but still, I am filled with apprehension. I try to understand them, how long they've waited for this, how glad they are to have me back, how much they want me to stay, but it does not change the fact that I am married to Henry. That I want to be with him more than I want to stay with them. It is a disheartening truth, but a truth nonetheless.

I am angry that they will not listen to me.

Father saunters in, looking as thin and pale as ever,

with his shirt tucked in tight and breeches shoved down into his tall, leather boots. His doublet matches the color of his hair. He also wears a crown, gold with a jewel in every crest. He must have been in a meeting, having never dressed so formally unless there was business afoot. "Redelia, Cornelia, may I have a moment with her please?"

All the women step out of the room, and Mother closes the door behind them. I am fearful, with his heavy gaze staring down upon me. It is stifling for some reason, and I want to ask him to open the window, but I do not open my mouth.

Pacing, he says, "There is something you should know."

If he wants me to ask him what it is, he will have to wait. I am in no mood to talk.

He stops, placing his hands on the footboard of my bed. "I will always love you, my child. And I hope you will visit us often."

He speaks louder now, his face toward the door. "You may let him in."

The door opens, and in steps Henry, not a vision in my dream, not an illusion of the mind, but the real, live king of Fallund. He does not smile, but I would not expect that, not from Henry, and especially not in front of my father, but I cannot contain my own joy.

"May I have a moment with her?" he asks solemnly.

"A *brief* moment," Father answers, retreating once again, but I think he leaves the door open a crack.

Henry approaches the bed, standing near the far corner. "How are you?" He seems hesitant. Is he afraid I do not remember? That it was all in his dream and the real me had no part in it?

"Awake. And infinitely happy to see you."

He lets his teeth show, allowing the biggest smile I've seen on him yet to overpower his straight face. After rounding the bed, he sits beside me, hesitant once more.

"Well, aren't you going to kiss me before Father comes back?"

He leans forward, pressing his lips to mine, and the sensation is unlike anything I've ever experienced. His lips are not the flavor of mint leaves, and not quite so soft as rose petals, but they are inviting, and filled with firm emotion: joy; longing; passion; relief.

A hot tear falls on my face. I open my eyes as he pulls away and see the clear tears falling down his cheeks. "I thought I had lost you forever," he whispers, resting his forehead against mine. "For days I tried to find you . . . figure out where you had gone. When I finally got word that you were awake, I sped across all of Fallund and Cray, all the while rehearsing what I would say to your father when I got here."

Father clears his throat from the door and Henry jerks away from me, promptly removing himself from the bed and standing beside me as if a soldier, legs together, arms clasped behind his back, chin out. I hadn't even heard the door open.

"He has consented for us to marry," Henry says, his lips in a firm line again, although I'm pretty sure he winks at me after saying it.

"Yes, but I could always change my mind." Father sends a threatening glare Henry's way before stepping inside further. "Dinner is being served downstairs. Would you like to join us, Eglantine?" His voice is full of hope.

"Of course, Father. But only if I get to sit by you." Turning his nose up at Henry, Father spins around and leaves us alone once more, but the door is left open this time. I try to let go of the fact that he listened to Henry and not me, and it is easy when I focus on the thrill of having Henry here; it swallows all else.

"Let me help you." Henry's strong arms help me to sit up.

"I don't think I can walk." I am anxious to try, but

doubtful.

"Stella has been exercising your legs every day. I'm sure with a little help you will be fine. Allow me to put my arm around your waist." And he does, lifting me until I am standing beside him. Flying would be easier, but from now on, I will have to learn to walk.

18
BEAST

Duncan leaned over the well, reaching down deep to catch the bucket before it got to the top.

"You're not very patient, are you?" Ovinia asked him, her hands still on the rope she'd been pulling a moment earlier.

"No." Smiling at her, Duncan marveled at how far she'd come over the last several months. The thing he loved the most, was how chatty she'd become, and not just to him. At first she'd been shy to meet the villagers and shop owners of Gilmuck. Duncan had secured them shelter, and found himself work as a scribe and messenger for several local professionals. Each morning Duncan made his rounds, asking if there was any work that day, and there always was. He'd never been so grateful for his castle education, having long ago mastered spelling and pristine handwriting. At first, Ovinia had stayed at home, walled in alone, but with time she'd asked to join him, and they often walked through the dusty streets together. It had been weeks since her last nightmare.

"Look," she said, pointing to the south. "Someone's coming."

Duncan scooped a ladle full of water and gulped it down. Looking in the direction of her pointed finger, Duncan squinted to see a man racing toward them on a determined horse.

Ovinia looked at him. "Who could it be?"

"I don't know." Duncan thought of the possibilities, but one seemed most likely. "Perhaps it's a message from the castle."

"The castle?"

His brother had given him total freedom, never having sent word at all since he'd left. And Duncan was grateful for that, knowing letters addressed to and from the castle would raise suspicion, intrigue, gossip and rumors among the locals. Grateful the people here knew so little of the royal family, Duncan wondered if his secret would be found out someday. How could he explain having the same face as the king of Fallund?

The horse approached quickly, and when near, was pulled to a slower gallop, then a trot, then an abrupt halt. He jerked his head back, obeying his master.

"Worston," Duncan whispered.

"Hello, Prince Duncan."

"Please don't call me that here. Or anywhere. I'm not a prince anymore."

"Don't be so snippy. I've only come to deliver a message." He swung one leg to join the other and stepped off the animal.

Stupid Henry. Why couldn't he have sent Karl? Perhaps he found him too old to make the journey. Or perhaps this was his way of punishing him from a distance.

"You're looking well, your majesty."

"Stop that or I'll disassemble your smile," Duncan warned.

"Isn't this the man who tried to bribe you when we . . ." She stopped, as if afraid to say the word 'escaped.'

"It's all right, love. You don't need to be afraid of him."

"I'm not. He looks cowardly. I think I might bite off his ear." Not only could she be chatty, but she often said the most shockingly humorous things.

Duncan let out a laugh as Worston took a step backward.

"Why don't you go in for a moment, love." Holding onto her elbow, Duncan kissed her cheek. "I'll take care of him."

"As you wish, but if you need any help just holler."

She looked as though she did not believe Duncan could handle it alone.

Amused, he answered, "I will."

"She's . . . charming."

"Yes, isn't she?" Duncan sat on the brick wall of the well and folded his arms across his chest. "So what's this all about? What is the reason I have the honor of a visit from Fallund Castle."

"The king is getting married."

Duncan thought about what this might mean. He couldn't tell Worston about the previous wedding. Was Henry marrying someone else? Poor Eglantine. "What do you mean?"

"What do I mean? He's getting married. What else could that mean?"

"Let me rephrase this then, since you're obviously too dull to catch on. Whom is the prince marrying?"

"Eglantine. Of Cray. Ring a bell?"

"But she's asleep."

"Don't you get word of anything up here?"

Duncan considered that, suddenly feeling isolated. "No, not much." It was true. The people from Gilumck traveled little, having everything they needed right here.

Worston held out the invitation, and Duncan

slipped it from his hands, carefully opening it.

"Dear Brother," it began. "I would be honored if you and (I forget her name) would join me on my wedding day. I will be marrying Princess Eglantine of Cray, who has miraculously regained consciousness. Hoping to see you, Henry."

Completely surprised, yet overjoyed for his brother, he asked, "When is it?"

"Two weeks from tomorrow. And he also wanted me to tell you that he'd love it if you stayed in the castle."

"Thank you, but we will stay at an inn along one of the rows."

"So you're going then?" Duncan hated the smile on his face, as if he had some wicked plan, or perhaps it was that he was so smug he couldn't help it.

"What? Why are you smiling like that?"

"He told me he'd pay me double if you agreed."

Ah, so he'd been gloating. He really was the worst sort of man, and Duncan was glad when he straddled the horse once more and turned to leave.

"A wedding?" Ovinia asked after Duncan went inside and showed her the invitation. Proud at how well she was learning to read and write, Duncan watched her examine it herself . "At the castle?"

"It will be all right. I'll be there with you." Duncan hung up his hat and vest and washed his hands in the little tub of water sitting on top of the wooden chest that held their firewood. He found himself preoccupied still with how it was all possible. The witch had told him she would sleep forever, that since the king and queen of Fallund had never produced a son, there would never be a brother to free Ovinia. And if there ever had been, it would have been too late.

After finding a cloth to dry his hands with, Duncan looked at her. Still crestfallen, and suddenly silent, he watched her stare out the window, as if in a daze.

"Or we could stay here. I would love to go, and love for you to come with me, but we don't have to."

"It's not that." Snapping out of her trance, she looked to him once more.

"What is it?"

Bowing her head, as if ashamed, or perhaps hesitant to speak the thoughts in her head, she waited a moment before answering, and when she did, spoke softly. "I don't belong in a castle."

Duncan wrapped his arms around her as she looked up at him and joined in on the embrace. "Well, not dressed like that, you don't. You'll need a fancy dress and flowers and ribbons in your hair."

"We can't afford those things."

He began shifting her in a slow, side stepping movement, back and forth, and spoke softly, reciting a poem they'd learned the night before. Poetry had been something they'd discovered together. Next to having her hair brushed, and perhaps even more soothing, it was on top of the list of things that she loved. "Remember nothing, only this, Before you fail, before you falter, With love's unbending tender kiss, you shall not change, you cannot alter."

She stared up at him for a time, lips together in a serious line, eyes contemplative. "I'd be happy to go with you," she whispered, resting her head against his chest.

* * *

The journey to the castle had been pleasant, Duncan and Ovinia having slept most of the long ride. Thankfully, since Henry had sent a carriage, he'd sent it at night, and to their knowledge they had gone undetected by the nosy villagers of Gilmuck.

Creaking to a stop in front of the inn along an

Eastern Row, Worston yelled, "Last stop for Prince Duncan and . . . Lady Ovinia."

Duncan's loathing for him would never cease increasing. He was sure of it.

"Pipe down or I'll crack your jaw," Duncan muttered through a false smile once off the carriage as he glanced around to make sure nobody had heard the announcement.

"And I'll rip your eyes out of your socket," Ovinia added, also sporting a large smile.

Duncan burst into a brief laugh.

Glowering at them, Worston asked if they would like a ride to the castle when the time came.

"No, thank you, Worston. I'd rather vomit," Duncan said, still smiling.

After watching the servant curse under his breath, the former prince deduced he must have been promised a fair sum if he'd convinced them to take a ride back to the castle. Hoping Henry would not be too ashamed of them arriving by foot, Duncan took hold of Ovinia's hand and led her into the Inn where they could drop off their belongings before heading to a dress shop.

Once out on the street again, Duncan gripped Ovinia's hand and led her down Western Corridor, allowing her to stop and marvel at the tiny window displays or the tables set up outside. She refused every offer Duncan made to purchase something that had caught her eye. "I'm just looking at it," she would say. "Looking is enough."

As they entered the dress shop, Duncan's jaw fell when he beheld the face of Magnolia, the witch who'd cursed Eglantine, Ovinia's mother. She appeared different in almost every way—her countenance lighter, her skin almost radiant, the old floral dress and cloak gone, replaced by a clean, soft blue linen frock and white apron, her hair pulled back.

After giving him a look of glad surprise, she approached them.

"Searching for a dress?"

"Yes, ma'am," Ovinia said.

Magnolia walked to her daughter, measuring her upper back and the line from her shoulder to her waist, and then from her waist to the floor. "What is the dress for?"

"It's for the royal wedding," Duncan said, keeping a close eye on the woman as he continued to wonder why she was there, and if it had been by coincidence or her own devising. He thought it strange to see her dressed in only a plain floral dress without the usual black cloak.

"Oh, how lovely," she crowed, standing tall once more. "I'll be back with a few choices."

Relaxing somewhat when she returned, Duncan retreated to the front of the store, glancing back at them every once in a while as they conversed or if Ovinia wanted his opinion.

Other than the color, Duncan could barely tell one from the other, but he liked the dark purple the best. Keeping his opinion to himself, he allowed her to make the decision on her own, stating that he liked them all.

Ovinia chose the dark gray one, and Magnolia wrapped it up for them. "Have you made arrangements for her hair?" the woman asked.

"No, do you have any recommendations?" Duncan inquired.

"May I do it?" The small older woman locked eyes with him, and Duncan could see how much she wanted to, how much hope she carried in her heart. "Please?"

"I don't mind," Ovinia stated.

"If you'll step into the back room, I have a small vanity." She gestured with an open hand to the door.

Looking around the room, Duncan could see she had planned for this, or at least hoped. Several combs and brushes rested on the vanity desk, as well as a bowl of tiny, white flowers and two spools of ribbon—one white and one the exact dark gray of the dress.

Ovinia glanced at Duncan through the mirror as she sat down, a small smile on her brave face.

Magnolia grabbed a brush and started to work it through Ovinia's hair. Mesmerized, Duncan studied the scene: the look of love and gentility on the old woman's face, Ovinia's smile and occasional laughter at something the woman said, the gradual coming together of braids, ribbons, flowers, and swoops of hair, the tenderness of a mother giving her daughter whatever she could, no matter how meager.

Upon leaving the shop, Ovinia remarked about how kind the woman had been. Magnolia had seen them to the door and urged them to come back again.

"Do you mind dressing at the castle?" Duncan asked. "It will save your new gown from soil and give me the chance to visit with Henry before the ceremony."

"Will it be all right?" Her brow furrowed with worry again.

"Of course it will, my love. Remember, this is my former home, a place where I am sure we will always be welcome."

Careful to avoid Northeast Alley, and any memories associated with the prison there, not to mention any possible confrontation from the guards, Duncan led her to the castle.

"It's beautiful," she said, pausing once inside the front garden gate and looking up at the tower.

"Not the grandest castle in the world," Duncan remarked. "But it's enough."

After locating Marie and asking her to help Ovinia get dressed, Duncan found Henry standing before a mirror in his room. "Hello, Brother."

Henry stopped fastening the buttons on his velvet doublet and rushed to embrace his brother, patting him heartily on the back in the process. "I'm so glad you've come." Henry pulled away slightly, only enough to look at his brother while still keeping a grip on his arms. "Did you bring the girl?"

"Ovinia."

"Right, I knew that," Henry said, finally releasing his hold. "Did you bring Ovinia?"

"Of course. I couldn't have left her alone."

Henry returned to the mirror to finish adjusting and arranging his hair and attire. "You know, the two of you could tie the knot while everyone's gathered." Henry gave Duncan a playful smile through the mirror.

Duncan picked up a seashell from the writing desk against the wall, examining it for a moment. "We're already married."

Henry scoffed. "That's funny because I don't remember receiving an invitation."

"Well, I didn't want anyone to know. That is, I'm afraid of the people of Gilumck finding out I'm a prince. I don't want them to think me a coward. Besides, our landlord would not rent us his place unless we were married." Duncan returned the playful smile, setting the seashell back down.

"Well, allow me to give you a gift then, in honor of your lovely bride." Coming away from the mirror, Henry approached his brother once more. "Take the carriage Worston brought you in. A carriage is a great asset to such a small village."

"Oh, we couldn't do that. Besides, the people would get suspicious. Scribes do not earn enough to purchase carriages."

Frowning, in the expert way only Henry could, he tried to convince his brother otherwise. "There is no shame in renouncing what you do not love. But please remember you are my brother, part of my very soul. Take the carriage. Do not worry so much if people know who you are. Please keep me with you as you press forward in your new life."

"What would we do with a carriage?"

"Come to visit once in a while." Upon seeing his pleas were not working, Henry persisted with a threat. "If you do not, I will send Worston to check on you every week."

Straightening his back, and pretending as if none of this conversation had happened, Duncan replied, "I change my mind, we'd love the carriage."

"I thought so. Thanks for coming to say hello. It's almost time. Meet me in the ballroom?"

Duncan descended the tower stairs, and upon peeking in the ballroom, found Ovinia standing with Marie at her side. Blessed Marie! Duncan couldn't imagine leaving Ovinia alone in this room full of people. Taking in the sight of her, Duncan found it hard to believe he had ever preferred the purple dress.

"You do belong in a castle," he whispered in her ear once he reached her side.

Ovinia's cheeks radiated a hint of warmth after, and Marie excused herself to return to the food preparations.

Duke announced the arrival of Henry and asked everyone to take their places. When an aisle had cleared, and all chatter had stopped, Duncan got his first glimpse of Eglantine since that day on the battlefield when she'd only been a vision. Wearing an ivory, jeweled dress, her hair a cascade of curls down her back, she walked with the queen of Cray on her right arm, and the king on her left. Duncan mused over how tragic this must be for them, to lose the daughter they'd lived without for so many years. Both of them had tears streaming down their faces, and seemed to find it difficult to release her into the waiting arm of the king of Fallund.

Duncan thought the short ceremony appropriate, since it was only a technicality after all; he'd witnessed their first wedding with his own eyes. But what caught his observation the most, was Henry. Usually so proud, so serious, so stern, he looked completely changed as he stared into the eyes of his new bride, and then cupped one side of her face before slanting down to kiss her.

After the stillness of that moment, a slow-rising din began to echo throughout the room, followed by louder conversations and the clanging of glasses. Ovinia, having held fast onto Duncan's arm through the entire thing, bravely slipped away, promising to return in a moment with drinks.

In her absence, Eglantine approached him, looking everything like the queen she now was. Her warm smile crept under his skin, finding a permanent place in his memory, heart and soul, in only the way a sister's could.

Awestruck by the idea of having a sister, he smiled back at her, adding a little wave. Suddenly he realized how it had come to pass, how Eglantine had been released from the curse. She'd married Henry just before he'd set Ovinia free. Henry had provided her with a brother after all. Feeling even more fond of her, and glowing with a satisfaction that he'd been the one to release her from the clutches of the curse, he reached out to receive her with an embrace. Eglantine approached him, nodded gracefully at first, and then smacked him on the shoulder.

Duncan checked on Ovinia to make sure she had not seen (or if she had, was not about to attack the queen) and found her speaking to one of the servants who held a tray of half full wine glasses. Returning his attention to Eglantine, Duncan asked, "What was that for?" It hadn't really hurt, but had been an insult nonetheless, especially given his new realization.

"That was for always ignoring me just because you couldn't see me."

"I didn't *always* ignore you," he began to argue, a chuckle escaping his lips.

"Don't . . . make me hit you again."

Duncan put his hands up. "Okay, you win."

Henry joined them, sipping on a glass of wine and

interlocking arms with his new and improved bride. "What have you won, darling?"

"I've won me a brother," she said.

Duncan smiled at her comment, then turned his head toward the exit, where a woman slipped out just before the door closed shut. Though she wore an elegant blue dress and had pinned up her hair, Duncan knew it was Magnolia.

"Excuse me for a moment," he said, rushing after the woman. Catching her softly by the elbow, he asked "Why have you come?"

Turning around to face him, she smiled and answered softly. "I just wanted to see her one more time. I didn't think you'd have much call to come back to the dress shop from here on out. I was lucky to find employment there. How I'd hoped you would bring her when I heard about the engagement." She took a moment to glance back at the wedding party. "It's strange, isn't it? That Eglantine's awake. I wonder if it happened because I gave up my status as a witch, denouncing the practice and taking off my cloak forever."

Duncan pondered this momentarily, but held fast to his theory about Henry giving her a brother who freed the woman's daughter. "Well, you're always welcome in

Gilmuck."

"Thank you. Perhaps I could visit now and then. Take care of her?"

"Of course."

Magnolia reached for his hand, gave it a loving squeeze, and then left the castle.

Returning to the ballroom, Duncan witnessed Henry introducing Eglantine to Ovinia, wondering if they'd ever realize, if he would ever come to tell them of their history, their bond through the curse, how they'd helped each other to freedom. For now, it was enough they were all at last a family.

The end.

Acknowledgements

I am so grateful to God for His help in writing this book. I truly feel like He has been there every step of the way. Special thanks to my family for their encouragement and support, especially my husband for his help formatting because trying to format a book is sort of like summoning a one way ticket to the insane asylum. I could not have done this without my amazing beta readers Misty Pulsipher and Amy Johnson, and my proof readers Jamie Carrier and Sharee Morrey. I would also like to express appreciation to Cindy Canizales for her beautiful cover design work. Finally, I am so grateful for family, friends and fans who continue to encourage me to write books.

About the Author

Melissa Lemon is the author of *Cinder and Ella* and *Snow Whyte and the Queen of Mayhem.* She lives in Maryland with her husband, three daughters and cat named Matilda.

Visit Melissa on the Web:

http://www.melissalemon.com/

https://www.facebook.com/authormelissalemon

http://lemoninkwell.blogspot.com/

CPSIA information can be obtained
at www.ICGtesting.com
Printed in the USA
FSOW03n1537061216
28249FS

9 781499 788808